MAUI TIME

A Novel ▪ Kay Hadashi

Honolulu ▪ Los Angeles ▪ Seattle

The Island Breeze Series

▪ ▪

Island Spirit

Honolulu Hostage

Maui Time

Big Island Business

Adrift

Molokai Madness

Ghost of a Chance

Maui Time. *The Island Breeze Series.*

Fourth Edition, January 2020.

ISBN-10: 1502348675
ISBN-13: 978-1502348678

www.kayhadashi.com

Chapter One

In the dark room, June Kato flipped the thin blanket off and struggled to the edge of the bed. She found her favorite old threadbare T-shirt and slipped it over her head, running her hands in gentle circles over her firm, round belly. Instead of stepping down to the floor, she kept her legs folded under her.

"We need air conditioning in this house." She rubbed her face. "Or deliver this kid."

June looked at her third trimester belly and yawned.

"Just two more weeks," she said quietly in the dark room. "And you insist on using my bladder as a beanbag chair, don't you?"

Dressed in an old T-shirt and cut off sweatpants, and armed with a flashlight and old broom, June padded barefoot out of the bedroom into the hallway, the yellow beam of the light sweeping the floor ahead of her. The old hardwood floors creaked with almost every step, but she had lived in the small plantation-style house long enough to know where to step for the least amount of noise on the way to the bathroom. In the hall, she scanned the floor with the light, the broom at the ready. As far as she could see, the way was safe and clear, all the way to her destination.

It wasn't until after her stop in the bathroom, the first of many expected for the day, that she found an unwelcome guest in the living room.

"Oh, there you are. I knew one of you guys had to be in here someplace," she whispered in the dark, as her soft beam fell on some movement. The little creature scurried toward the safety of the underside of the couch, but June got to it first. “You’re a big one, too.”

Using the broom like a hockey stick, she kept the scorpion trapped under the bristles while dragging it to the front door. While jockeying for position to get the door open past her belly, the scorpion broke free and skittered away.

“Hey!” she whisper-shouted. Leaving the flashlight behind, she went after it in the dark house, floorboards creaking under her bare feet. “Come back here, you little…”

She cornered the tan scorpion in the kitchen. She got the door open, and with just one flick of the broom, the scorpion went flying out into the moonlit yard. Her morning project done, June leaned the broom against the breakfast table and put a kettle of water on the stove to boil.

“Good morning,” her father said, walking into the kitchen. It had become the rallying point for the three people that lived there.

She turned on the coffeemaker when she saw him and dumped a packet of instant oatmeal into a cheerfully decorated bowl. “Hi Dad. Sorry if I was noisy.”

“Should’ve let me check the floors for you,” he said, after gently squeezing her shoulder. He grabbed a papaya and began preparing it in his recently adopted breakfast: slice it in half, scoop out the seeds, plunk in chopped pineapple, and squeeze a lime over top.

“I can do it.”

“You need your sleep. You’ve been looking tired when you get home from work lately.”

“Thanks for the compliment. Everybody at the hospital is tired after work. Eight months pregnant doesn’t make it any easier.”

"Should you be working so hard?"

"Dad…" She poured her father a cup of coffee and joined him at the table with her oatmeal. He already had a bowl of papaya ready for her, along with a glass of guava juice. "Worry about something else."

"How much time are you taking off after the baby comes?"

"Dad, leave my career alone."

"I'm more concerned about your health."

"You already know the answer. There's no need to ask me the same thing every morning."

While her father dug into his fruit with enthusiasm, June complacently stirred her oatmeal. All she had an appetite for was juice, drinking his once she was done with her own.

He nudged her half of the split papaya to in front of her. She looked at with disdain.

"How's the addition coming?" she asked, staring at his steaming coffee. Her mind begged for a cup of it, but she was determined to wait out the last two weeks of pregnancy before indulging in any. Other than giving up on daily runs and saying goodbye to her fashion model figure, coffee had been her greatest sacrifice in the last several months.

"You haven't gone back there to look? The windows are in, siding is on, and the roof is done. Today I'll put up the wallboard, and tomorrow start mudding it. On the weekend, I'll sand…"

"Whatever," June said impatiently. She pushed her uneaten oatmeal to her father. "I thought it was only supposed to take a few weeks to build. It's been months."

He pushed the oatmeal back to her. “Construction always takes twice as long and costs twice as much as originally planned.”

“And that’s another thing. Money isn’t growing on trees around here, Dad.” She tried eating a spoon of her oatmeal, but it went down in a lump. “Will the dang thing be done any time soon?”

“You’re teaching the baby to swear like that.”

“I think we already know what the baby’s first words are going to be.”

“Did you talk to Jack about getting some money to help with the addition?” her father asked.

“It’s my house, not his. He’s the one who updated the house when I first moved in. I’m not asking him for more.”

“When was the last time you talked to him?”

“Yesterday. And before you ask, he called me.”

While June’s mother had accepted the unusual relationship between June and the baby’s father, her father hadn’t been so generous. Jack was as wealthy as he was busy. June’s father always maintained, though, that it would only a moment to write a check or transfer money from one of his many bank accounts to hers.

“Did he propose?”

June sighed. “Dad, please leave it alone.”

“Why don’t you let your mother and me help with some money? We’ve lived here right from the beginning and you’ve never once asked for rent.”

June went to the kettle for more water in her oatmeal. “Because you’re my parents. You never asked me or Amy for rent while we were growing up in your house. How could we?”

"You're that determined to do everything on your own? No help at all?"

"Dad, if you want to pay rent, move into Amy's house and pay her. I'll be glad to give you a ride to the airport."

She took her juice glass to the giant jug of filtered water, filling it to the top. When she sat again, the papaya had been pushed back in front of her, a spoon next to it. She begrudgingly ate a scoop of the soft papaya and some of the crushed pineapple, knowing she would only get nagged if she didn't.

"Sorry, I didn't mean to say that. Just sort of grouchy lately."

"Should've seen your mother when she was carrying you and Amy. Sailors and ex-husbands have words to describe women when she was like that. How'd your OB appointment go yesterday?"

"Had my last ultrasound. Everything is normal for Jim or Jane, whoever is in there kicking me all the time."

"You don't want to know the sex of the baby?" he asked.

"It's not twins. That's all I care about."

June had a twin sister Amy, five minutes older than her. Amy also had twin daughters. As much fun as it was growing up as a twin and having twin nieces, June didn't want twins of her own. At forty years of age, and as a single mother, one kid was going to be enough.

Her parents had been living with her right from the very beginning, moving to the resort area of West Maui from Los Angeles where the family was from originally. It was only supposed to be temporary, at least until the baby came and June was back to work. The addition onto the back of the old house was a large bedroom and bathroom, meant as a master suite. But June could already see how her parents were digging in for the long haul. She had moved to the island at the same time the baby was conceived. For that reason, June's history on the island was forever intertwined with that of her baby and her job as neurosurgeon at the medical center.

In the dimly lit kitchen, they chatted about baby names she had considered. It was still a wide-open topic, with potential mainstream names like Mike, Bob, or Jack Junior, or possibly Japanese names like June's real name of Junko. Still another possibility was a Hawaiian name, something sweet and feminine if it was a girl, or masculine for a boy, something June was leaning toward.

"You need to sleep more, Dear," said her mother, Mabel, shuffling into the kitchen. "And eat more than that."

June took another scoop of the fruit, not feeling the necessity.

"How much did you weigh at yesterday's appointment?" her mother asked, settling at the table.

"I've gained a pound since last week."

"That's only eighteen pounds," her father said. "Shouldn't it be ten pounds more?"

"Yeah, Dad, I should be ten pounds fatter." June pushed up from the table, leaving the last of her breakfast behind. "And my clinic should be busier, my surgical schedule should be fuller, and the patients should have better insurance." She drank a glass of water and turned for the door toward the rest of the house. "On the other hand, there shouldn't be scorpions living in my bathroom, a never-ending construction project on the back of the house, or nagging parents shacked up in the spare bedroom."

Normally preferring a cold shower before going to work, June had got into the practice of warm showers during the latter parts of her pregnancy. Her bathing ritual long over, she let the water stream over her body, slipping her hand over her belly.

"Come out pretty soon, okay?" she said, looking down at her belly. Other than her breasts, her belly was the only part of her that had grown in the last couple of weeks. She had eaten as much as she could right from the beginning, but the morning sickness was too much at times, and lasted far too long. But right then in the shower, there was nothing she could do but have the only private moment she could afford all day. By the time she turned off the water, she couldn't tell the difference between a few tears and the shower spray streaming down her face.

***

"I'm making a bug guard for the doors," her father told her on the way to the hospital.

"Don't worry about it, Dad. They'll get past anything. Just get the mudding done today."

"Wallboard today, mudding tomorrow."

"Whatever," June said, looking out the window of her pickup truck. It was the vehicle used by her dad for trips to the hardware store. She had over an hour to fill with rounds on only one patient before her scheduled case in the operating room was set to start. She hoped the cafeteria would have some buttery hash browns, and doubly hoped they would stay down this time unlike the day before.

The sky was bright and the sun strong by the time June's father let her out at the main entrance of the growing medical center in Ka'anapali, located on the dryer side of the island.

"Eat lunch today," was the last thing she heard before slamming the pickup truck's door closed.

"Yeah, Dad, I'll just take a break in the middle of a six-hour brain surgery so I can go have lunch," she muttered as she went in the hospital.

***

June watched as potatoes were diced up on the greasy griddle. Bacon and sausage was grilling nearby, turning June's stomach before she even got her food on a plate.

"You're getting big, Doctor Kato!" the young Filipina woman said while working at the grill.

"Thanks. Normally that's not much of a compliment, but today it sounds nice, for some reason."

"When are you due?" the Filipina asked.

"Two weeks from tomorrow."

"Oh! Not big enough!"

"Doing the best I can," June muttered. "Maybe your cooking will put on another pound or two."

June got her plate of potatoes and found a table where someone had left behind a newspaper.

The headline said it all:

SECOND MAUI SCORPION DEATH

A second West Maui woman has been found dead in her home, from an obvious scorpion sting. Following only one week after the first death, the woman was found in her Napili condominium yesterday by a housekeeper. And just like the first death, a sting puncture was found on the woman's wrist, a crushed scorpion on the floor, a cell phone just out of reach of the victim's hand.

"Probably be me next time," June muttered. "Maybe I should've taken Dad up on his offer to critter-proof the house."

She flipped to the next page of the newspaper, reading about national news, then more local news, followed by the island crime report. With each turned page, she managed another bite of the oily potatoes, pretending she couldn't taste the pork fat on them. She was a lifelong vegetarian and planned to remain that way. She had left a dozen notes in the cafeteria comments box, requesting a separate grill for making truly vegetarian meals. So far, no luck.

She scanned meaningless scores on the scanty sports page, before returning to the front page to read about a new high school being considered for her part of the island, the school her kid would eventually go to. Also on the front page was a story about the President negotiating a nuclear truce between two far-flung Middle Eastern nations.

President Jack Melendez has returned to Washington DC from the Central Asia Summit, a copy of the bilateral denuclearization agreement between two enemy nations. Both nations have six months to comply...

"Jack saves the world from nuclear armageddon while I battle poisonous bugs with a broom."

She went back to where she finished reading about the dead women with scorpion stings.

According to the police, the woman, whose name has been withheld until her family on the mainland can be notified, was a new resident here on Maui. Police investigators are working to piece together information from her neighbors, the housekeeper, and what they found in the woman's condo. From all indications, the woman's death will be listed as accidental, and the preliminary reports from the coroner at the scene support that.

She took out her cell phone and tapped on a number she was beginning to rely on too much.

"Yeah?" her father said in a sleepy voice. Instead of working on the house, he'd been taking a nap. "You okay?"

"Fine. But maybe you should make that bug screen like you said, okay?"

"Why? What's going on?"

"Another scorpion stinger death. It's in the newspaper. How's the addition? Getting some work done?"

"Yeah, just getting started. Hey, maybe it's time to start killing those little buggers?"

"Not killing anything in my house," she said, wondering why she even called him.

"Kill the adults and you eliminate the next generation."

"You're saying that to a pregnant lady, Dad. Can you just figure out a way of keeping poisonous wildlife out of the house, please?"

She ended the call and went on rounds, seeing her one and only patient in the hospital. He had spinal surgery two days before, a car accident victim while on vacation. She accepted him onto her service directly from the Emergency Room and was able to do surgery that very same day, and his improvement reflected that.

"I'm still so surprised you were able to do his surgery like that," the patient's wife told June. Every time she made rounds on the man, the wife seemed more interested in the pregnancy than her husband's recovery. "When I had our kids, I spent the entire last trimester on the couch."

"I wish I could spend more time relaxing, but my folks are visiting, and my dad is adding on a room to the back of the house. Noise all day long." She forced a smile leftover from her ancient fashion modeling days, even letting her dimple flash for a moment, something that didn't show very often in the last few months. “These days I come to work just for the peace and quiet.”

“When are you due?”

“Two more weeks, which I can tell will be an eternity.” She went to the head of the bed where the patient was listening. “Mister Jensen, you will be home to Wichita by then!”

She set her hand on her belly, feeling another kick.

“Are you okay?” the wife asked. She had stepped over to June’s side.

“Just more kicking.”

“My mother always said that lots of kicking was better than no kicking at all,” Mrs. Jensen said.

“Raising a ballet dancer?” the patient asked.

“More like a kick boxer.”

She put the woman’s hand on her belly. They both smiled with the next kick.

“It means an energetic child. Who knows? Maybe you’ll raise a surfer.”

“Yep. Plenty of those on this island.”

After changing into her surgical scrub clothes, she sat on the toilet one last time, trying to squeeze out every last drop. She had already checked on her patient, a lifelong Maui resident and elderly man with a tumor near the center of his brain. It was what she had trained for, and her reputation as a neurosurgeon was centered on the advances she had made in deep brain surgery. Her hospital schedule had been full, even overflowing, in Los Angeles before moving to Maui. Now after several months, patients were still just trickling in.

June washed her hands and looked in the mirror. “Game time, June. Whatever that means anymore.” She looked at the shirt stretched over her pregnant belly. "And when I said get born soon, that doesn't mean in the next few hours, okay?"

June went through the same surgical routine she had a thousand times before, until it was finally time to sit in the chair she would use while working through the microscope. In only a few months time, she had got a team of nurses trained up to the demanding standards required for the type of surgery she was doing that day. Maybe because of their efforts, or just because she could take her time with no other patient waiting for her, she didn't mind if there was the noise of conversation while she worked.

She listened to the nurses as boyfriends were discussed and tried to remember a couple of the recipes they mentioned. Having a basketball under her shirt made surgery more difficult, slowing her pace, making the case much more tedious. Maybe the hardest thing was the baby making its presence known by giving her an unexpected kick every now and then.

There was a lull in the conversation when someone came in to give the nurse a break.

"Did you guys hear about that new scorpion bite?" the break nurse asked. Not only was she a career smoker, she was someone not on the team personally trained by June. From what June could tell, she seemed to talk more than work.

Scorpion bites were something June definitely didn't want to hear about. The hillside up from the house she had bought was being graded for a new residential neighborhood, forcing scorpions out of the rugged landscape and into new hiding places below. With no other houses around, her place was the first shelter the little creatures got to during their daily exodus, and almost every day another scorpion had to be shooed out with broom and dustpan.

"The one in the newspaper this morning?" June asked.

"Another one today. Here in the ER right now."

June pushed back from the surgical microscope and looked up.

"Who is it? Did you see them?"

"Some white lady. New Age looking. You know, those baggy pants and wearing a caftan."

"You mean a mu'u mu'u?" Dr. Miller, the anesthesiologist, asked.

"No, a big tent. Don't they call those caftans?"

Feeling bad for the woman, but knowing it couldn't be someone in her family, June went back to work.

"She's still alive?" Miller asked.

"Yeah, looks in bad shape, though. I think she's going to the ICU. I wonder why these women the last few days are dying?"

"They've all been women, right?" someone asked.

"All three are ladies recently from the mainland. Pregnant, too."

June looked up again at the news this latest victim had been brought to the hospital alive. "This latest one is pregnant?"

"The one in the ER a few minutes ago looked pregnant."

"What do you suppose it is, June?" Dr. Miller asked.

"I don't know. Scorpion stings usually aren't fatal. Unless the ones here are particularly venomous?"

Aida, the scrub nurse, took over the conversation. "Years ago, my grandparents and parents worked in the cane fields here, and they all got stings one time or another. Bad news, hurts like heck, but back to work after a couple days off. No big deal for them."

June kept picking at the tumor, working with the microscope, reaching far over her belly. "Could it be related to pregnancy?"

"My auntie got stung once, while pregnant with my cuz. She was fine. Cuz is weird, but okay," Aida said.

"Weird?"

"Not sick kind weird, just silly boy, you know?" Aida Hernandez, fourth generation Filipina on the island, the first to go to college in her family, was letting her local pidgin accent shine through. "You're having boy or girl, Doctor Kato?"

"I don't know. Just want a big surprise."

"Who's your OB?" Dr. Miller asked.

"Divya Gill."

"Oh, you're having your baby here and not at the mall?" The anesthesiologist asked about the other, larger hospital on the island built decades before.

June had heard the history of the place several times from nurses at work. A civic center had been planned for the small city on Maui then, with a new city hall, post office, county courthouse, police headquarters and jail, along with the hospital. Even a small shopping mall was planned to be only a few blocks away. By the time the hospital was nearing completion in the first phase of the large project, little money was left for the remainder of the buildings. Instead, the mall was built, and much larger than originally planned. Over the years, it had grown into a full-sized shopping complex, and ever since, the hospital nearby was known as the 'mall hospital', or to West Maui Med employees simply as 'The Mall'.

"Yes, why?"

"They stay plenty busy at the mall." June could hear her friend known as Millertime tapping on his monitors, getting a paper readout of something. "And Doctor Gill is…mmm…"

"Young?" June asked.

"Well, yeah."

June smiled, knowing exactly what Miller meant. Her OB had finished her residency training only recently. "So were you and I once, Millertime. Plus, she trained at the same place I did in LA, specifically in high-risk pregnancies, which to a certain extent I was toward the beginning. Have you worked with her much in the OR?"

"She does a nice job with her surgical patients and the few deliveries I've witnessed," Miller said.

"She's fantastic," Aida added. "If I was going to have another baby, I'd go to her."

"Well, if she's good enough for you, she's good enough for me." June had checked out her OB's qualifications thoroughly at the beginning, talking to old friends back in LA, and wouldn't have backed out this late in the game anyway.

"Do you have anesthesia picked out yet?" Miller asked.

"Divya keeps harping at me to find someone before she assigns someone. I'm scheduled for Monday two weeks from now. Are you volunteering?"

"You're not going natural, are you?"

"Are you kidding? No way in the world I'm pushing a basketball out my basement door without some help."

June sat back, and handed the last of the pearlescent pink tumor to the scrub nurse. She was done with the most difficult part of the case and it was time to begin reassembling what she had taken apart.

"I'm not on duty that day, but I'll be glad to come in to do your epidural."

"I've seen you put lumbar drains in a couple of my patients, and if you can do that, you're more than welcome to do my epidural." June took one more look through the microscope after dribbling irrigation into the deep tunnel before swinging the scope out of the way. "Good! One less thing for Divya to worry about. Now, if I can just figure a way of keeping the scorpions out of my house, I'll be a happy girl."

***

By the time she was done with the case, June was spot on her six-hour time estimate. Mid-afternoon was a quiet time in the hospital, when most patients were back from having procedures or therapy appointments and were getting rest. She took advantage of it by seeing her patients, going her clinic to check on the next day's schedule, before having a bite to eat in the cafeteria.

Pushing two slices of bread into the toaster, she burnt them, the only thing that actually tasted good anymore. After the toast and tropical punch, she made one last quick trip to the bathroom. With a trip through the Emergency Room to see if it was busy, she got the name and ICU room number of the woman with the scorpion bite.

June looked in through the glass panel that separated the patient in her cubicle from the rest of the world. She recognized the nurse taking care of her as a trustworthy regular in the department. She could also easily see the patient was still very much pregnant, and with a fetal heart rate monitor attached to her.

"Not in good shape," the ICU nurse told June when she came out of the cubicle.

"How's the baby?"

"Apparently, she didn't have an OB, but was going natural at home with one of those so-called birth angels."

"Birth angel?" June asked.

"I've seen ads for them. Sort of a New Age type of person who helps with deliveries."

"You mean a doula?"

"From my understanding, doulas are mainstream compared to these so-called birth angels. Doulas have training, but when I looked up birth angel training online, there wasn't much. I guess it's just too new as a profession for anyone to know about."

June remembered reading a recent newspaper article about this latest type of birth practitioner, followed by advertising in a few of the local magazines. From what she could tell, they were neither mid-wives nor doulas. With no professional licensure but still considering themselves health care professionals, they created a new term, of the so-called birth angels, New Age women dedicated to helping others through their pregnancies, but at a cost. With their new label, they persisted in their claims of a 'safe, natural, and wholesome delivery in the privacy of the mother's own home'. They advertised as though they existed only to help the financially needy, but catered to wealthier women coming from the mainland.

"Someone found her down in a luxury Napili condo and brought her to the hospital. I guess she wasn't breathing on her own at the time of arrival. One of our OBs came by to evaluate, and the baby seems to be doing well. No decells or whatever on the heart rate monitor, anyway."

"Whatever that means."

Ninety percent of everything June knew about maternity and obstetrics she had learned during her own pregnancy, and mostly through experience and learning after the fact what it meant. There really couldn't be a bigger chasm in medicine than between obstetrics and neurosurgery, something she was glad about.

With one last glance at the unconscious woman hooked up to a ventilator to assist her breathing, June turned for the exit. Once outside in the warm sunshine, she pulled out her cell phone and called home for someone to come pick her up.

In days gone by, she easily would've walked or jogged the mile trip home. She almost felt like walking, just for a few minutes of time alone, but in the tropical sun and humidity, and a kick boxing baby inside her, she went with the prudent thing to do, or at least wouldn't get her scolded.

"How was your day?" her mother asked once June was inside her parent's new sedan. When they moved to Maui, her parents had bought the largest sedan they could find, something big enough for June to easily get in and out of while pregnant. She got herself situated and the seat belt across. "Fine. Did you hear anything about another scorpion bite?"

"No. Just the one in today's paper."

"There's been another, this morning, and not far from here."

"Did she…" her mother began to ask.

"She's alive in the ICU, being treated for anaphylaxis. But she hadn't been breathing for a while." She went on to explain the definition of anaphylaxis as a severe allergic reaction to a foreign substance introduced into the body that is often fatal. One of the biggest initial problems with anaphylactic shock was the cessation of breathing efforts. Lack of oxygen to the mother was bad for her, but even worse for the baby. June looked out the window, trying to avoid eye contact with her mother on the short drove home. "The thing is, she's pregnant."

"The baby is…"

"Still okay, I guess. They're watching the baby as close as the mother. She looked nearly full term."

"What if the mother…" Mabel started.

"Dies? They can take the baby out by emergency C-section." June kept watch out the window as they went up the long bumpy driveway to her house. She tried in vain to keep a tear welled by an eyelid. "No dad."

"What? How can there be no father? Where is he? This isn't the Sixties anymore."

"Um, hello? No dad at my house, either."

"It's different for you. You have us, and Amy. Jack, eventually."

"If Jack comes through with his promises. With each passing month, I believe him a little less."

"Never mind that. Tell me about the girl in the hospital."

June explained what she had learned that day, about women coming to Maui from the mainland to have their babies in a New Age way, with the help of 'birth angels', eschewing traditional medicine for something labeled as natural, even mystical.

"What's wrong with that?" he mother asked. "Women have been giving birth for thousands of years without doctors or nurses."

"Yes, but there's always a village expert around to help. The question is if they're getting competent pre-natal care. The way it sounds, they're turning it into being all about a woo-woo experience for the mother and not about a healthy birth of a baby."

"It's not something for you to worry about, Dear. You just keep focused on your own baby."

"I know. I am."

"Don't turn this thing with the birth angels into one of your crusades."

June couldn't get out of the car quick enough. As soon as she walked in the back door of the house right into the kitchen, she was surrounded by the pungent aroma of garlic. Her dad was at the stove, and she lifted the lid off the pot, stirring a long wooden spoon through the vegetable broth. June knew it was for her, that garlic was one of the favorite flavors, and something her stomach could manage in larger amounts. Heavy ramen noodles would be tossed in a moment before serving, but she needed the bathroom and a change of clothes before sitting down to a meal.

"How did the mudding go today?"

"Mudding is tomorrow. Wallboard was today and it went well."

That's when she heard hammering at the back end of the house. She also realized the term 'addition' had been upgraded to 'new room' lately, probably in an effort to appease her impatience.

"Who's working in the back?" she asked.

"I hired a guy to help out."

"Dad, I really don't want strangers in the house. We still haven't been here long enough to know who to trust."

"You won't mind this kid."

"Dad..."

"Just go to the new room and meet him."

June didn't like the idea of having a stranger in the house, especially left alone. She got a surprise when she got to the new room, the ceiling and walls covered with new plasterboard, small pieces littering the floor, a few tools lying around in the thick layer of dust

"Rodney!"

The young man quietly set down his hammer and faced her. "Hi, June."

June glanced around the room again before going to him. Rodney was the brother of a friend, June's office manager from her old job in LA, and a friend in his own right. Mildly autistic, he worked at June's small organic farm on the outskirts of LA. He was strong as an ox, worked hard all day, and was as trustworthy as anyone June had ever met. He just never had much to say. She gave him a quick, one-handed embrace. "I bet I look different now?"

"Becky said you're going to have a baby."

"Very soon. But I'm so surprised to see you here."

"Vacation. Becky and her boyfriend came here, so I came here with them." He looked worried but tried to smile. "It's okay, June. Someone is doing my work for me at the farm."

June recalled then that Becky had told her a few weeks before about her vacation plans on visiting Maui with her new boyfriend. June didn't expect to see them much while they were here, maybe once for dinner. What June hadn't expected was that Rodney would come with them.

"Well, good. But why are you helping my father with his work instead of sightseeing?"

He seemed to blush. "Becky and Kyle want to be alone. This is more fun than sitting at the beach all day."

"It probably is. Are you eating dinner with us?"

He squirmed as though he hadn't given dinner any thought. "I think they have plans."

June smiled as she led Rodney from the room. "I'm sure they do, but you're welcome to eat with us every time you help my dad."

June went back to the kitchen after changing her clothes, where Rodney was already at the table where a large bowl of stir-fried vegetables sat with a plate of bread. The noodles and hot broth were ladled into bowls and brought to each place setting.

"Everything got done today," her father, Tak, said.

Taking a spoonful of the soup, June flicked her eyes up at her dad. She wondered how much he had actually done, or if Rodney had done all the work. She still hadn't heard anything about how much he was being paid.

"What I saw looked good," she said. "Rodney worked hard all day."

"We had a hard time convincing him to eat lunch with us," Mabel said.

"It's okay," he muttered, struggling with his chopsticks to eat the soup noodles. "This is different than the farm."

"And tomorrow the walls get finished?" she asked.

"Get mudded. After they dry, they need to be sanded, remudded, then sanded again."

"How long does all that take?"

"One day each."

She let out a sigh, unable to keep it silent. "When does it get painted?"

"Next week."

"How long does that take?" she asked

"Three layers of paint, one day per layer," her father said, stirring his broth.

"Is there dust when you sand?"

"Yes, but we'll sweep and vacuum each day when we're done. Right, Rodney?"

He nodded his head.

"That's not what I'm worried about. I'll bring home surgical facemasks for both of you to wear to keep the dust out of your lungs. You promise to wear it, Rodney?"

He nodded again.

"The two of you actually know what you're doing out there?" she asked. "I mean, running a flower business and working on a farm is one thing, but building a house is something different. Maybe not so easy as what they show on TV home improvement shows?"

"All the structural work is done. What's left is cosmetic, walls, paint, trim, the floor." Her dad held up a thick stack of papers he was working from. "Everything has been done according to Maui County code. Got all required permits and inspections. Otherwise, one day at a time, as they say."

"Please don't burn down my house, Dad. In spite of the creaky floorboards and giant scorpions, I like it here."

"What are you so crabby about, anyway?" her father asked.

"Oh, I don't know. Eight and a half months pregnant, hotter than heck, and forget about the humidity. I haven't had a cup of real coffee in months, no appetite, and I'm still trying to perform delicate neurosurgery while the baby uses my bladder as a trampoline. Anything in there that might indicate why I might be cranky?"

The remainder of the dinner topic of conversation, as it was quite often lately, was about the scorpions that were invading the house. Once that was quickly exhausted, June finished off a second bowl of noodles with the vegetable and garlic broth. There was something related to the scorpions that was troubling her. Leaving the others to make a phone call, she sat in her bedroom for privacy.

"What do you know about these so-called birth angels, Henry?" she asked. Henry was a friend she'd met on her first visit to Maui, a nurse who worked at the hospital Emergency Room. He and his wife Karen had a new baby, and June figured she would be learning about childcare by watching them in the coming years.

"Them specifically? Not much. But Maui has been attracting New Age types for many years, semi-retired divorced ladies trying to escape something in their lives back home. Bad marriage, messy breakup, aging faster than what they expected. Maui has become something of a tropical Sedona."

"What do they do for work?" she asked. "Maui's too expensive to just hang out. Unless they're independently wealthy."

"Usually not. Mostly they act like hippies, crashing on someone's couch or basement. Sooner or later, they get married, move back to the mainland, or get a job. Some end up homeless living on the beach."

"What kind of job does being a lazy New Age retro-hippie get you?" June asked. "Because back in the day, being real hippies got them nothing."

"Some sell real estate. Others sell pot."

"I can see selling real estate, especially in this market. I've never understood how people can possibly earn a living selling pot. How hard can it be to grow the stuff? Put a seed in a pot of dirt, give it some water and sunshine, and a few months later, they can get high for free."

"Condo dwellers, I guess," Henry said. "Anyway, what I've heard at work is that this latest rendition of birth assistants call what they do 'intuitive medicine', or 'intuitive healing'. I've seen a couple of their clinics in town."

"What do they mean by intuitive medicine?" June asked.

"They claim it's an off-shoot of holistic medicine. Less intrusive and more mystical. Sensing auras, manipulating energy, that sort of thing," Henry explained. "As a doctor, do you think there's any basis for it?"

"You're asking a traditionally educated and trained brain surgeon what she thinks of New Age concepts. I rely on clinical evidence and research to guide my practices," June said, looking through her dresser drawers for something cooler to wear than the T-shirt and shorts she'd changed into. "I'm also Buddhist, and many New Age concepts were pulled from Buddhism and Hinduism. What bothers me about it is that people tend to adopt the things they like or are easy to believe about a religion and discard the ones they can't be bothered with." She knew her ire was up and she was beginning to vent steam. "Sorry, Henry. I guess I get tired of people raiding my religion for what they can get, but when the chips are down and they're looking death in the face, they kick Buddha to the curb so they can go to Heaven."

"Setting aside religion, do you think there's anything to it from a scientific standpoint?"

"Generally, if it can't be proven through research studies and closely-monitored trials, western medicine tends to ignore it. What these birth angels offer doesn't seem based on science, but I don't know much about them yet."

"Well, what's the difference between that and acupuncture, massage, and chiropractics?" Henry asked. "You have to draw the line somewhere. And lots of people swear by acupuncture and chiropractics. Even you have to admit there's something to alternative medicine, June."

"Because those have been studied and have shown value. Anyway, the Chinese have been using acupuncture for thousands of years, and that's one heck of a big trial population. That means the difference between alternative medicine and some of the New Age healing stuff is that there have been no monitored clinical trials of their techniques. Also, what's the training? Who says someone is trained properly? Is there licensure for intuitive medicine?"

"But if it doesn't do harm, what's the big deal?" he asked.

"How does a pregnant woman know harm won't be done? Has she been getting legitimate checkups by a qualified practitioner? If there's a problem with the birth, is the intuitive practitioner able to deal with it?"

"They could call an ambulance to take the girl to the hospital."

"Which brings intuitive medicine to a close, replaced by western medical practices, and by delaying treatment, adds risk to the mother and baby," June explained.

"That's a good point. But to play devil's advocate, what's the harm if the mother is healthy? I mean, women have been giving birth for a million years without the help of doctors."

"And until these last hundred years or so, the mortality rate for all those births was much higher. Evidence shows that the live birth rate is vastly higher in regions with competent medical practitioners as compared to places with predominantly home deliveries without the attendance of a qualified practitioner. As far as I'm concerned, that's the point of maternity care, for the delivery of live births, and not for the mother to suffer fetal demise. Are they getting vaccinations? Vitamins? Is the pair of scissors used to cut the cord sterile?" June pulled her shirt off and tugged on a tank top, something that used to reach her beltline but now barely reached her belly button. "Let me put it this way. Let's say your car is running well. You take the whole thing apart using only one wrench, then put it back together again. Will it run better or not by the time you're done with it?"

"I take it to a mechanic for maintenance," he said.

"Exactly. Things turn out better when someone is educated and trained to do the work."

"But we cook our own food rather than eat in restaurants where chefs work."

"And you don't poison yourselves because you know how to cook the meals you eat, or at least follow a recipe. You've learned how. But not being trained chefs, how would complex meals turn out if you tried cooking through intuition in a restaurant?"

"You have a point."

"Right now, my father is building an addition onto the back of the house, with some help from a friend. Neither one of them are architects or contractors, but so far, no problems with inspections. Why? Because they're going by county codes, following plans drawn up by an architect, and using the proper tools. At least, I think they are. Even though I give him crap every day when I get home from work, I can tell the project is going well."

"Maybe because you give him crap every day."

June laughed. "Probably."

"You have me convinced," Henry said. "Getting back to the original topic, the latest birthing fad is for women to come here to have their baby through intuitive birthing. Apparently, some go through the in vitro fertilization process elsewhere, before moving here to have their baby."

"Which is about as much fun as…" June let it go. "But do the women stay after giving birth?"

"Sometimes. But I heard of a daycare center opening somewhere in West Maui that will cater specifically to that population. It's funny, though. A lot of them chicken out at the last moment and come to the hospital. We've had a few come through the ER in early labor looking for a budget OB."

"Proving my point," she said. "In spite of coming here for some sort of spiritual birth experience, they eventually look for a western-trained practitioner. Once again, sorry. And yes, I know I'm looking at it from a very narrow mind, but I think childbirth needs to be safe for the baby's sake. If somebody wants religion, they can go to church or temple and pray for a while."

"A whole little community has grown up around this," Henry explained. "There are the birth angels, and counselors, therapists I guess they are, and like I said, the daycare centers. I even heard a rumor about plans for some sort of colony where they can all live together."

"Sounds more like a cult," June said.

June had heard enough about what she was beginning to call sham practitioners. Snake oil salesmen for pregnant ladies. Going back to meet the others, the sky had gone dark, and the only light on in the house was in the kitchen where they were. She was told Rodney had gone home to the suite he was sharing with his sister and her boyfriend at the resort directly across the road.

"I gotta go pee. Can someone check the floor in the bathroom for me? That seems to be the latest hangout for the scorpions."

Her father Tak used the flashlight and broom for scorpion patrol down the hall to the bathroom, flicking on lights along the way. Once the bathroom had been cleared, she went in and locked the door.

"I'll start mudding the drywall," he told her from just outside the bathroom.

"Dad, I know it's a small house and it's all in the family, but I'd like a little privacy, if you don't mind."

***

June didn't like being naked while she was pregnant, but the evening temperature hadn't receded much since dinner, and the weather was intensely humid for May. Lying on her side, all she could manage were old cotton shorts and a sheet up to her waist. It almost felt like afterglow, but without the pleasure.

The house was small enough that they could almost carry on a conversation from one end to the other. What June didn't like were the bedtime discussions about thing that had been hashed out at the dinner table, or the pestering questions and demands of her parents. Most often it was about eating more the next day, getting more rest, or taking more time off after the baby came. They'd already been through all of that twice since dinner, so when someone knocked at her door, June had no idea what they wanted.

"Yeah?" she called out, pulling the sheet up to her shoulders.

"You want the fan tonight?" her mother asked, leaving the door closed.

"You keep it."

"You're sure?"

"Tell Dad to buy another fan the next time he's at the hardware store, okay?" she told her mother. "Maybe a couple more of the dang things. One for every room."

She could hear her mother's footsteps recede down the hall and the guestroom door close.

She flung the sheet off her body. "I won't be pregnant forever," she whispered. She rubbed her belly. "Right, Baby?"

Before she could doze off for the night, the baby wasn't done with her. With a hand on her belly, she felt movement at two different places.

"Baby's kicking and I gotta go pee again."

Wrapping in the sheet, she shuffled down the hall to the bathroom, checking the floor for giant bugs as she went.

"I wonder what happens when the baby comes? Do we have to sit guard duty at the crib to keep the bugs out?" she mumbled, waiting until she knew she was done.

Chapter Two

The morning in the clinic went like clockwork. One patient per hour was scheduled for June to see, about one third of what she was accustomed to in her old practice. But in LA, she had the help of a resident physician in training to keep the schedule moving. Having hour-long appointments gave her time to sit with each patient and thoroughly discuss her findings from physical examinations or X-ray studies that had been performed, along with prospects of recovery from surgery and physical therapy. It also allowed her to use the bathroom between almost every patient, something that was getting more tiresome with each passing day.

"Come out!" she implored while looking down at her belly during a trip to the toilet. She poked her finger at her belly button, now completely pushed out. She hadn't weighed herself since her last trip to her OB, but she knew she was bigger.

Before seeing her first afternoon patient, she went to the office manager, also one of her clinic nurses, and a new mother. Since she was the only neurosurgeon at that hospital, she had a small office and clinic, with only two exam rooms to use. June couldn't take much time off after the baby came, or she'd risk losing the minimal space the hospital provided. For that reason, her planned maternity leave was much more of a short vacation.

"Jesskah, have you heard of something called a birth angel?" June asked her.

"Oh, no! You're not thinking of that, are you?" the young woman asked. With blond hair slowly turning to dreadlocks and a dark suntan, she was better suited to hang out at the beach everyday than to work in a medical center.

"No, not at all. I was just curious about them. Could you do me a favor and find some sort of list of them?"

"I already have the billing done for the day. It would give me something to do."

"See if you can assemble a list of all mid-wives, doulas, and these birth angels on the island. I'd like to see if there's some sort of overlap in them."

"Oh, like if mid-wives are calling themselves something else, just to snazz it up a little?"

June felt a kick and tried to settle it by rubbing her belly. "That's the idea. Maybe that's all it really is, a way of relabeling themselves."

June didn't just want names and addresses, she had plans to visit one or two of them, and without her family knowing about it. If she told them, they'd insist on going along, if not trying to talk her out of it altogether. She was also curious about the counselors and therapists that worked with them, and the community they supposedly lived in. June had the image of a hippie commune in her mind, with stolen food and pot being smoked all day by pregnant women, hot tubs filled with flower petals and murky seawater, a public health nightmare.

If she worked it right, she might even be able to finagle the car from her mother for a while the next day, Saturday, a day off. She'd just need to plan her route with predictable restrooms along the way.

By the time June was done with her last patient of the afternoon, Jesskah had assembled a short list of five names, other than the legitimate mid-wives. None of their names over-lapped with the doulas or the birth angels, and none of the doulas were also listed as birth angels. June sat in her office and dialed the first number. Getting no answer, she tried the next. On the third try, she got a response.

"Yeah, hi. I'm interested in learning about the birth assisting you do," she told the woman who answered.

"Yes, my name is Marilyn Scanlon. I am a DIB, and have worked in the field for several years." She went on to give qualifications, and pretended to name-drop without actually giving names.

"DIB?" June asked.

"Doctor of Intuitive Birthing."

"I see. Where did you get your training?" June asked. Until just a couple of days before, she had never heard of birth angels, and never would've guessed there were doctors of it.

"It is a privately-managed online program with extensive, rigorous cyber-guided training." She went on into a lengthy explanation of her training, using a lot of words to provide very little content.

"Uh huh."

"Of course, we only work with women on their own," the woman told June.

"On their own?"

"No men," the woman said. "We find that a women-only environment brings out the goddess experience in our followers."

June could hardly believe what she was hearing, the complete opposite of what she was planning for herself in the hospital. She was planning an epidural in clean and safe surroundings, with competent practitioners prepared to manage any complications that might arise. Trying not to pass judgment too soon, she wanted to find out if they were truly qualified mid-wives who put a religious or spiritual slant on childbirth. To get more information, she played along. "I see. Yes, that's what I'm looking for. But the thing is, I'm due quite soon."

"When?"

"A couple weeks, I guess."

"That is soon." There was an audible sigh and a pause, and June could tell the woman was writing something. "We would have to start quite soon to fully develop your consanguine relationship."

Consanguine was an unusual word, even for medical professionals, and June wasn't sure if it was a real word at all. All it would mean was the blood relationship between mother and child, most likely while the baby was still in the womb. She decided to press for more. There were two ways of keeping the woman's attention, flash the promise of money or sound pathetic. She went with the cheaper route first.

"You see, I was with an OB back on the mainland, but…" She tried to inject a little pathos into the tone of her voice. "…I think he tried to take advantage…you know?"

"Oh, you poor thing."

"Can you see me? I've heard there are counselors that can help?" June asked pathetically. "I can pay cash at the time of services rendered."

After making an appointment to see the woman the next day at noon, she learned that one of the main methods of consanguine therapy was massage, something to expect in her appointment.

There was something oddly suspect about this new method of maternal healthcare, and the more June heard about it, the odder it sounded, and the more she wanted to know. It was going to be something of an adventure, learning about this new craze that seemed to be sweeping Maui, but at least she'd get a massage out of the deal.

***

"Your dad said he won't be noisy today, just working on mudding the wall," Mabel said at breakfast on Saturday morning. Rodney was already at the house, busy working in the new addition. "I guess he already has everything he needs, or whatever. I don't know."

"He's sure Rodney doesn't mind working here on his vacation?" June asked, pushing cold oatmeal around her bowl with a spoon.

"I think he's more excited about working in your house than being in Hawaii. All he did yesterday was talk about making a new house for you and the baby, how interesting it was for him. He could be painting a barn in the hot sun, and if it were for you, he'd be happy."

June put more hot water from the kettle into her oatmeal and gave it a stir. "Just don't let Dad take advantage of that. And he better be paying him pretty dang good."

"What are you doing today? Getting some rest?"

"I need to make rounds at the hospital and then go out for a while," June said, not feeling the energy for it. It was going to be a hot day and she was already sweating that early in the morning.

"What for? Shouldn't you rest?"

"Just an appointment. Not far away."

"What for?" her mother pressed.

She wasn't going to lie to her mother, but withholding information wasn't out of the question. "I'm getting a massage. I think it'll help me relax. It's from someone that works with pregnant women, so it'll be okay. It's in

Wailuku, so I need to go early to find the place. I still haven't learned my way around central Maui."

It was true that she didn't know the streets of Wailuku or Kahului, two towns joined at the hip that made up the small city on Maui. On the rare occasion she went to the central part of the island, she mostly drove straight through to go to the mall or airport. From her standpoint, there wasn't much difference between the two towns, except one had narrow meandering streets with older plantation-style homes similar to hers, and the other had more of a modern gridwork type of layout with subdivisions of hurricane-resistant cinder block houses.

"You need one," Mabel said, washing the breakfast dishes. "Give me a few minutes so I can drive you."

Sprawled knock-kneed in the kitchen chair, June used a handful of napkins to mop sweat her face and neck. "I can drive myself."

"You barely fit in the front seat of the car."

"I want to drive myself so I can aim all the A/C vents at me. Don't feel like sharing today, Mom."

"I don't mind."

"Actually, you know what?" The only thing about the trip in the car she was looking forward to was the A/C. "I need a little time alone."

"It does get a little crowded around here. Once the new room is done, we'll all have a little more space and privacy," her mother said. "Be careful driving through the tunnel. There was another accident near there last night."

"I know." June yawned. "I was at the hospital doing surgery on one of the victims for half the night."

"I never heard you go out or come back in."

"I got back right before you guys got up. Rodney was already on the front porch waiting. Dad better be planning on giving him a bonus when he goes home."

"Did the patient…"

"Survive? Yes. A full recovery is still questionable."

"I don't know why you do all that work," her mother said, starting the dishes. "Long cases, middle of the night, terrible situations."

"Because it's my job. I'm the only neurosurgeon on the island willing to work cheap and take care of those patients. The neuro guy at the other hospital on the island refuses most trauma or low reimbursement cases. Ambulance crews have learned to bring all neuro patients to West Maui Med because somebody here will take care of them."

"I'll never know why you do all that."

"Would it be better if I let them die?" June asked, wondering why she was allowing herself to be sucked into the same old argument.

"It just seems like you're doing a lot of free work since you moved to Maui, Dear."

"I did a lot more of it in LA. You never knew because you never saw it. Now that you live with me, you and Dad are discovering the life of a neurosurgeon." June tried pushing up from the table but couldn't get the right angle to do it smoothly. Instead, she eased down into the chair again. "I was a heck of a lot busier then than I am now. That's why I moved here, just to get out of that environment and get a little more time to myself."

"Well, you need to sleep for a while before you go out."

"I will."

"And get a shower. You smell a little strong this morning."

"Thanks for the compliment, Mom."

June went off to shower and then to bed, setting her alarm for an hour and a half before her massage appointment time. After her nap, she took another cold shower before dressing. Looking through the house, only Rodney was there, quietly working by himself, filling gaps in the walls with gray mud.

"Looks great, Rodney. You're working hard."

He stopped what he was doing to face her. "Thank you, June."

"You don't mind working by yourself?"

"Your father said I can be my own boss."

"You always are when you work at the farm." June wondered where her parents went, leaving him to work alone. There was something terribly unfair about someone on vacation working alone on someone else's house. "Wouldn't you rather be at the beach or visiting some tourist places?"

"This is fun. I like building the house for your baby."

"You're very sweet, Rodney." That made up June's mind about how much he was going to get paid. "I have to go out. The kitchen is all yours. Help yourself to something to drink or eat."

As usual, he only waved, going back to his work.

"This is Dad's project, not Rodney's," she griped going to the car. She felt bad about leaving him alone, just to do work. "The kid's on vacation, after all."

It took some work, getting the seat and steering wheel adjusted so June could fit into the driver's side with a small measure of comfort and still reach the gas and brake pedals. As she was stretching the seat belt across her belly, she reconsidered the wisdom of driving herself, and thought about waiting for her mother to return home to drive. But this was a mission she was undertaking alone, something to satisfy her curiosity. It wouldn't take long, a simple trip into town and back, and there was the prize of a massage for doing it.

Once she was in the town of Wailuku, she pulled off to the side of the road and looked at the map. The street she wanted was one of the few straight streets in town, one she'd been on before, an older commercial street. One and two-story storefronts were covered with corrugated metal roofs, many with awnings or extended rooflines over the sidewalks. Most of them were tiny mom and pop type stores and small diners, the kinds of places her parents would patronize. She too had begun discovering the value of smaller businesses, if for no other reason than the friendly customer service and spirit of independence she found in them.

Walking the length of one block, she passed by a coffee shop, the aroma of roasting beans greeting her nose as she passed by. Once again, it was tough to deny herself caffeine. She made a mental note of a few of the businesses, planning for return visits.

She found the place she wanted in an older wooden building, a small shop with a sign painted on the front window: *Pandora's Women's Health Center*. Still early, she went past to sit on a bench the next block down. From her clutch, she got an elastic band and put her short hair in a stubby ponytail to keep it off her face and neck.

"Pandora?" she muttered. "What's that supposed to mean? She had a box of gifts for all of humanity, but also a box of troubles that was never supposed to be opened. Seems like a weird name for a health care clinic."

Feeling the sun shining on her legs was only making her hotter, so she went to her appointment early. Inside was a recirculating waterfall that made a cheerful tinkling sound, and soft Zen-like music. On one wall was a poster of a nighttime sky constellation, one she didn't recognize, with an overlay of a Hawaiian folklore figure, something else she didn't recognize. The walls were painted in various muted pastels, and two chairs sat along one wall turned to face away from the front window. A doorway was in the back wall, with floor-length strands of beads functioning like a 1960s style curtain. The beads gently clacked from the breeze that came in with June.

A middle-aged woman with an overgrown buzzcut and dressed in a billowy green caftan sat behind a desk off to one side. Sleeveless mu'umu'us were popular in Hawaii, but they were different from the heavy fabric, tight neck, and long-sleeved outfit the woman was wearing. She stood and extended her hand.

"Are you Aiko?" The woman's smile was a bit overdone. June gave one of her own. It sunk in right then she was in the lion's lair, the cave of the anti-Christ to modern medicine. For that reason alone, June had given a false name when she made the appointment, an old alias that still came in handy from time to time.

"Yes, that's right," she said, tossing a tiny accent into her voice, and raising the pitch slightly.

"You're Japanese?"

"Not anymore. Are you Marilyn?" June asked, purposefully stumbling over the 'R' and 'L' in the name.

"Yes. Some people call me Doctor Scanlon. But please, call me whatever you're comfortable with." She seemed to make an effort to speak slowly.

June made a point of looking back at the Pandora's sign in the window. "Pandora? Interesting name."

"Seems appropriate, somehow." Marilyn showed June through the beaded curtain into another room in back, the beaded strands clacking maniacally when they passed through. "I'm not sure if it pulls women in or keeps them away. But I've found it's the Goddess in a patient that comes to see me."

June was led to a small office with another desk, certificates on the wall behind it, potted palms in each corner, and small baskets of fake flowers and polished stones on corner tables. An old-fashioned medical exam bench with metal stirrups hanging down at the sides was partially hidden by a shoji paper blind. As far as June could see, the only medical thing in the room was the old bench.

Once they were settled, June got a closer look at the other woman. Her eyes were ringed with sky blue eyeliner, or maybe it was tattooed on, June couldn't quite tell. A pink bulbous mole sat proud of her cheekbone, the kind doctors like to remove to check for cancer. Because of the dress, all June could see of the woman's body were her hands and head. She couldn't shake the feeling there was something else hidden below all the fabric, something more than just flesh and bone.

Marilyn began. "How did you hear about me?" she asked, knocking June out of her assessment. "I don't recall what you told me last night."

June had come prepared with answers, and with her phony accent. "Word of mouth. Your name is quite prominent here on the island. But I'm not sure of the difference between what you do and what a doula does?"

Marilyn smiled. "I can explain later. And your interest in birth angel assistance?"

June sat knock-kneed in her chair, the only way she could sit comfortably. She ran her hand over her proud tummy, making slow circles. "Well, pretty soon I'll need some help. But like I said last night on the phone, I don't trust those people in the hospitals." She almost laughed at the idea but barely controlled her grin. "And no men."

The admonition of 'no men' seemed to win points with Scanlon. Up to that point, the meeting had a suspicious tone to it. "Never any men, let me assure you. The birth of a baby is a Goddess experience. If the Phallus was meant to be involved, men would carry babies also."

Pandora, Goddess, Phallus. June wondered what was next.

She wanted to argue the point that a man was needed somewhere along the way, but that argument would get her tossed out. Goddess versus Phallus could wait for some other time. She was there for more information, not argument. To accomplish that, June played up the hurt, innocent role, by casting her gaze to her lap. Her fingers wrestled with each other all on their own. "I'm a little afraid…"

"Most women are afraid at first. But it is my role in the wonder experience to bring forth the Goddess, to let the power of the Goddess within to soar."

June began to grin, but forced it into a smile.

"But there is such limited time for us to work together. Only in two weeks, you say?"

June nodded.

Marilyn went to a long narrow table against one wall. June watched as she took four sticks of *senkoh* incense from a small box and lit them with a Bic lighter. Rather than waving them out, Marilyn blew the tiny flames out. With the first whiff, June could tell it was *mainichikoh*, or an everyday type of incense used in the home for remembrance of passed relatives, completely inappropriate for a health care setting. Next, she went to a basket and collected several small pebbles, carefully selecting them one at a time with careful consideration. Back at her desk, she took a piece of parchment paper, the type used for baking, from a drawer and arranged it flat on her desk. With a hint of pomp and circumstance, she silently muttered something with her eyes closed. After, she gave the pebbles to June.

June glanced at the four narrow streams of pungent smoke rising from the *senkoh*. It gave her the creeps. "Four sticks of incense? Why four?"

"Yes. Different number for different women. I can tell you're a four."

June got chicken skin, the tiny hairs on her arms standing up. She tried rubbing them down again. "Why am I a four?"

"You exude four, even when you walked in through the door, I told myself, 'That woman is a four if there ever was one."

June clutched her bag and considered fleeing. "I only ask because the number four to the Japanese is, well, avoided."

The number four was pronounced with the same sound as death, in both Japanese and Chinese, and both nationalities were particularly sensitive about it. To somewhat superstitious June, it was like black cats, broken mirrors, walking under a ladder, and Friday the Thirteenth all rolled into one.

Marilyn tried smiling away June's comment. "Go ahead and cast those stones of prediction onto the sacred parchment, Aiko."

She tried not to react with a roll of the eyes or shrug. She dropped the pebbles on the thin, brown paper and watched as they settled.

"What's this for?" June asked.

"To see if you have the essence of the coming sky."

"Oh." June flicked her eyes up to Marilyn's face to see if she was serious. Superstition was one thing; parlor tricks were something else. "What about the sky?"

"The sky is full of energy, and affects us in many ways. Most people don't realize that."

"And that applies to my pregnancy somehow?" June asked.

"You don't know? A comet is coming, and will be visible only from the middle of the Great Amnion. That is very fortunate for the Child in you."

Any undergrad biology student knew a fetus is suspended in amniotic fluid inside the womb. "The Great Amnion?"

"Most people know it as the Pacific Ocean. The comet will pass through the sky in a few days, and Maui is one of the few places in the world where it will be visible. If the Child makes its transformation during the Crossing of the Comet, the Wondrous Event will be a miracle."

June was getting tired of her baby being called 'the Child' and the birth called a 'Wondrous Event'. Pain was going to be involved, even with an epidural. Now, a comet was crossing through the Heavens very close to her due date, something she had heard nothing about, and Marilyn was turning it into a miracle. And the Great Amnion? It almost sounded as if the whole thing was being made up as Marilyn went along. June smelled a rat, a very expensive one.

"What do the pebbles tell you?" she asked.

Marilyn rearranged the pebbles a bit, coming up with a satisfactory pattern. "From eighteen stars cast from your hand, I needed to move only four."

"Oh?" There was that number again. But once again, it came from Marilyn re-arranging the stones, not from fate.

June couldn't believe she was paying cash for a lowbrow tarot card reading. But if it led to something useful about how the scorpion stings were related to the dead pregnant women, and if these so-called birth angels were connected, she could endure. A massage was a part of the deal, after all.

"Anything less than half predicts a wondrous event. For you, it was less than a quarter of them." Marilyn smiled again, a perfectly practiced commercial smile, something that would've been pretty twenty years earlier, or at least in a more sincere setting. "You are probably wondering what the Crossing of the Comet has to do with this?"

"Yes."

"Are you familiar with the Hawaiian star sign of May? It is hoku welowelo, the comet, a shooting star." Marilyn posed dramatically, one hand aimed at the ceiling. "Such tremendous luck for you to give birth during this month. You shall have a child that will be the living embodiment of a shooting star. So lucky for you!"

"I see." But June didn't. "Does that have anything to do with why there are so many scorpions running around these days? Do they somehow sense the comet coming?"

Marilyn seemed shaken by the question, one that maybe she wasn't prepared to answer from a prospective client. "No, not that I'm aware of. Why do you ask that?"

"I read about those women who died from scorpion stings. I think they were pregnant."

"Nothing for you to worry about."

"Well, what were the pebbles for?"

"They were a diagnostic tool for the practitioner, not for the patient. They represent something very difficult to understand."

June spilled a little more accent into her voice and stirred it into the Ls and Rs. "Can you tell me exactly what it is that you do during the wonder event?"

While Marilyn used a pencil to circle each pebble's position on the parchment, she explained. "Yes, just exactly what do I do as a birth angel? One of my primary duties during the event is to assure a moment of peace. I've found lots of encouragement is needed, and when the moment finally comes, to keep Goddess and Child together, warm and wondrous. If your Child lives up to being a comet, it will arrive very quickly when the time comes."

"I see." June chanced a glance at her watch. "What exactly do you do at the moment of wonder?"

"In the days before the arrival, I guide mother and baby through their transformation to Goddess and Child. When the wondrous moment finally blesses them, I manage the moment's aura."

"Aura?" June had no idea of what to say. "I'm looking forward to it. But I'm still curious about all the scorpions on the island lately. With the comet on its way, it seems like they're related somehow." Her next question was a risk but she had to ask. "Do you use scorpions during the wonder event?"

Again, Scanlon seemed taken aback with the question. "Why would someone ask something like that?"

June was disappointed that she wasn't any closer to learning if the recent scorpion stings in pregnant women had anything to do with the birth angels. Between Greek gods, a flying comet, and sticks of funerary incense in a medical clinic dedicated to birth, the whole thing was weird enough without scorpions being involved. "Just a coincidence, I guess."

"Are you ready for your massage?" Marilyn asked.

June bit her lip. She had heard enough for one day, and couldn't begin to guess what a birth angel massage might be like, if more pebbles were involved, or if fruit was used somehow. The burning incense inside the small room was making her eyes water. Mostly, she wanted to get away from the woman that was getting scarier with each passing minute. "Maybe I've used up too much of your time."

"It's part of our first session together. Just a simple countenance examination and aura massage."

"Should be okay. In here?" With another glance, she could tell the exam bench wasn't big enough to act as a standard massage table.

Marilyn went to the bench and slid open a step to the front.

"Keep your clothes on. Just remain on whichever side is most comfortable."

Keeping her clothes on was a measure of safety, anyway. She helped June up onto the padded bench, and then onto her side. A cotton sheet was spread over June from shoulder to foot. June kept her clutch in her hand, the only thing she had brought with her.

Marilyn began to hum, something of a melody-less background sound perfect for meditation. As sleepy as June could've been right then, she had dozens of thoughts going through her mind, most of which if the session cost was going to be padded somehow. She had agreed to the forty-dollar fee when she made the appointment, only because she was getting a massage out of the deal. But listening to Marilyn hum and moan, she would gladly pay extra if she kept quiet.

Finally, Marilyn's hands went to work. It wasn't a true massage, but more of a gentle sliding, swooshing effect with her hands over June's body.

"I'm cleansing your aura now."

'You're cleansing my wallet, it what you're doing,' June thought.

"You have trouble…"

'And it started when I walked in here.'

The hand flicking and swooshing across June's body became more energetic.

"The troubles are deep…I'll try to locate them…they are running, hiding from me…"

'Which is what I should've done an hour ago.'

After another twenty minutes, the aura cleansing and massage came to an end, Marilyn helping June upright again.

"Did you survive?" she asked with a broad smile.

June used a finger to wipe away a bead of sweat that was threatening to run down her forehead. "Mostly."

"Goddesses tell me that sometimes after their first cleansing. But you have some very deep trouble, maybe deep into your soul. I'd like to work with it one or two more times before your wonder event to help progression.." Her face changed when June didn't readily smile. "It would be best for Child."

June slipped down to stand on the floor, shifting her clothes back into place. She needed to think up a reason not to come back. Grasping at straws, she said, "I know I shouldn't tell you this, but I still have another birth angel to see. Later this afternoon, actually. I'll have to decide between the two of you."

"Oh? That should be fine. Who is it, by the way?"

June got out her personal schedule and pretended to check her calendar. She then pretended to check her cell phone for a number. "Rats, I didn't put her name in here, but she's over in Kahului. I have the address here someplace."

"Oh. You mean Katrina. She's still fairly new at this. But fully qualified, from what I've heard." Marilyn looked at the cell phone in June's hand and grimaced. "You know, all that technology emits rays of disorder, something that is not good for Baby."

June put the phone back in her clutch and took out the small wallet. She had two twenty dollar bills already at the top to pay for the treatment. She smiled when she handed it over.

"So, would you like to book your next session? I have a very affordable and comprehensive plan, that would include two more cleansings and the Wonder Event."

"First, I'd like a receipt, please."

"Reciept?"

"Yes, for the money I just paid for this visit."

"I can give you a receipt for everything after the event. Would you like to book your next appointment?" Scanlon insisted.

"Can I call you?" June asked, collecting a couple of the woman's business cards. Marilyn stuffed several brochures in her hands about birth angels.

Pushing out the door to the sidewalk, she thought she might call the woman, if just for more answers. But she needed to think of the right questions first.

***

Mid-afternoon was hot on the central Wailuku sidewalk, and June had to pee. Instead of going back to her car, she walked along the store fronts for a little window-shopping, hoping to find a place with a restroom. After only a block, the baby was beginning to kick, and June needed to get out of the sun. Half a block ahead was a shop she had seen earlier, a place she knew would have a bathroom.

June stepped into the small beauty salon and smiled. What looked a little shabby on the outside was modern and clean inside. The lighting was dim and fans were running. It almost felt like air conditioning was turned on.

"Hi Hon. Have a seat," the stylist said to her. There was only the one, and she had a young customer in a chair. "Someone will be with you in just a sec."

"Um, actually, could I use your restroom?"

The young stylist was blowing out the long hair of the young woman, neither of which were much older than teenagers. "Maybe you should. Right back there," she told June with the nod of her head.

Before leaving the bathroom, June looked in the little mirror over the sink. She was too pale for living on a tropical island, and her eyes were showing the fatigue of not getting enough sleep. She used one last paper towel to dry her neck and face before going back out again.

Originally, she only went in for the bathroom but considered lingering in the air-conditioned salon for a while. Her only other alternative was to go for a long drive in the car with the A/C blowing in her face. But the idea of having a shampoo with cold water and a cool blowdry sounded good. And she just wasn't ready to go home yet. She still had no idea of where her parents had gone that morning, and just didn't want to sit at home in a stuffy house. If Rodney hadn't been there, she could've stripped down to a swimsuit and rub ice cubes on her body to keep cool, but she wasn't going to put on a burlesque show for the kid. Mostly, she wanted to get her mind off what had just transacted in Marilyn's office.

She took a seat at the front and grabbed a dog-eared hairstyle magazine, listening to the other women talk over the noise of hair dryer, flipping from one page to another. It had been almost a year since she'd gotten her hair cut into a short pixie style, and not only had the style grown out but the highlights also, making her overdue for at least a trim. Even though the magazine was full of Asian models, none of them looked like her, and she had a hard time visualizing any of the styles on her. She found one that was cute, something she had considered once, and bent the corner of the page before tossing it aside. Mostly she was looking forward to cold water running over her head and the scalp massage that went with a shampoo.

She eavesdropped on the other women while thinking about some of the things Marilyn had told her. One of the oddest was the bit about the comet astrological sign. June knew little about Polynesian folklore, even less about astrology, and wondered if comets and falling stars were viewed as magical occurrences to Hawaiians. The thing about Marilyn was she appeared to be completely white, with no visible traces of Polynesian in her face or skin tone at all, making it seem odd that she would be so concerned with the spiritual side of the Hawaiian culture. June had already learned something about the different types of Hawaiian kahuna and what they are capable of from meeting one several months before, a relative of a patient. Could someone named Marilyn Scanlon possibly be a kahuna? And was the term 'birth angel' simply a translation from a Hawaiian word?

Just as she was getting tired of thinking about Scanlon and started looking at magazines again, the stylist finished.

The young girl with what June thought was overly-treated hair paid and left. After the floor was swept, June was waved over and seated. The young stylist introduced herself as Myong. Another stylist came from a back room and introduced herself as Kim, the owner and namesake of the salon. She seemed familiar to June, that maybe she'd seen her in the hospital at some point, maybe in the cafeteria or elevator. Once it was determined June was a new customer, Kim took a magazine of her own and sat in the vacant chair as though she was interested in whatever gossip June might have to offer. The whole thing felt friendly and homey, just like so many other small businesses on Maui. A long black and white checkered cape was tossed over June and secured. The stylist slipped the band from June's stubby ponytail, fluffing it. June felt a tiny drop of sweat forming near her hairline above her forehead.

"What can I do for you?" Myong asked. Her accent was a little more noticeable now.

June had a few qualms about allowing a teenager to work on her hair. "Ah, well, just a shampoo and blow dry.

Hot day, and when I saw your shop I thought it might be nice to have a cold shampoo."

Myong examined the ends of June's hair. "I could trim some of this old color if you like. Give it a little shape. Wouldn't take long, or cost much more. No more appointments today. But one thing I won't do is a chem process on a pregnant lady. Not good for baby, yeah?"

June took a lock of her hair in her fingertips, looking at it cross-eyed. She hadn't paid much attention to her hair or complexion since she'd started showing months before. Her bangs had reached her eyes and the hair in back was down her neck. The color still looked good, if combed the right way. She wasn't sure she wanted to go back to a pixie, though. "What would you do?"

"Thin the bangs, tidy the sides, cut the back blunt. I think a nice little bob would be cute on you."

June had never considered herself 'cute', even shuddering at the idea that she would try to look twenty years younger. When her twin sister had a bob years before, it had looked good on her. But as a supermodel, Amy knew how to carry it off, and that haircut had been done by one of the most expensive stylists in LA, not by a kid in a cheap salon on Maui. With nothing to lose, she made up her mind. "Yeah, let's do that that."

Even having her head sprayed with cool water was a welcome relief. While she had expected more work done on her bangs, nothing much changed there, and most of the work was done in back. In barely ten minutes time, the haircut was done and June was at a shampoo sink.

The shampoo was perfect, starting at a tepid temperature and getting cooler with each successive rinse. She got the scalp massage she needed, and could've easily have taken a nap right then. The only thing keeping her awake was the soccer game in her uterus.

"When is your baby due?" the stylist asked, rinsing June's hair.

"Two weeks from today," June told her. She lifted her hand with her watch from under the cape to see the time. "Two weeks from right about now."

"Boy or girl?"

"Surprise!" June said. The kicking settled a bit when she ran her hand over her belly.

June was taken back to her chair and she watched as Myong formed a different part at one side than what June normally had.

"I'm not married yet but my sister, she has two. She got one of each. Three and five. Both are blessings. But I'd have to know what I was getting before they arrived."

June explained how for two generations, it had been all girls in the Kato family line. She tried for the hundredth time to imagine how much trouble would come if a boy was introduced into the family.

"Twins run in the family, also." She sighed. "Thank goodness not in mine."

Myong chuckled. "Why?"

"Too many mouths to feed, too many diapers to change, too much crying, not enough quiet."

Not only did Myong laugh, but Kim did also from where she sat near the door. "Better not talk about twins too much or they might come anyway!"

"Yeah, don't invite company you don't want to visit your house," Myong said. June's hair had been combed straight. "Mind if I tidy a little more?"

June turned her head one way and another, looking in the mirror, trying to visualize something. "Maybe a little more."

Kim left her chair and wandered over to June a picture in a magazine. "This way very popular these days."

"Not much different than now," Myong said.

June had been in town for much longer than she expected, and was wondering if her parents were worried about her. They hadn't called, though. "Will it take long?"

Myong touched June's tummy. "Is there a hurry?"

June laughed. "You have two weeks!"

As Myong worked at removing almost nothing, June relaxed. Trusting the girl, she let her eyes close, and it wasn't long before she began to drift off. She had to wake herself up, or she wouldn't get any sleep at all that night.

"Do either of you know much about Hawaiian folklore?" June asked to distract herself from the slow-motion progress of the haircut.

"No local girl, eh?" Kim, the stylist seated in the other chair, asked.

June shook her head. Myong steadied it again.

Kim made a frowny face like she was deep in thought about something important. "Everybody here knows a little. What do you want to know?"

"What the Hawaiians think of comets and shooting stars."

The two stylists spoke in Korean for a moment, giving June a chance to look at Kim's face. More and more, she seemed familiar. Maybe it was the shape of her face, of soft but prominent cheekbones and a sloping jaw line that was common in the women in her family. The color of her almond-shaped eyes seemed most familiar, but the rest of her body was just too short and skinny to be a Kato. It was almost as if Kim had come from peasant stock and never had the better nutrition of later generations to help her grow bigger and taller.

Kim finally answered. "Back in olden times, the fishermen navigated by stars. Even cross the ocean, just by watching the stars."

"Nothing about shooting stars or comets?" June asked.

Kim shrugged. "Why?"

"I heard a comet is going to pass by, and Maui is one of the few places where it can be seen. I was just wondering if all the scorpions these days have something to do with that?"

"Those dang bugs! Just squish'em all."

"Yeah, maybe so."

Myong was working at the side of June's face, but stopped and appraised what she had been doing. Kim stepped over and inspected the incomplete style and gave some pointers to the younger stylist.

"So, have there been a lot of scorpions at your houses?"

Kim nodded at Myong. "That one lives in condo with parents. Just usual amount at our place."

Kim instructed Myong again on how to proceed as if it was a training session, Myong mostly ignoring her.

Kim took her seat again. "Should be clear night. Go look tonight. Squish'em outside before they get into the house."

"Maybe I will." June watched as Myong worked her way forward. She hated to micromanage what was happening, but she was the one who had to walk around with the style on her head. "Maybe not so short toward the front and soften the edge just a little."

With that, the chair was turned a little for Myong to work on the front, or maybe so June couldn't watch in the mirror.

That didn't stop June from asking questions. "Are there island legends or whatever about scorpions?"

"Nah. The Filipinos hate'm. Always get the sting in the cane fields. I heard once, scorpions only like Asian taste, not haole, yeah? Maybe Filipino taste best to scorpions? I dunno."

"I see." June doubted the scorpions tasted much of anything, since they stung with their tails instead of bite. June figured haoles, or white people, didn't get stung as often because they had better living circumstances and didn't work in the fields as laborers as much. "Seems like there's a lot of them lately."

Myong took her scissors, comb, and clips to the other side and started there, making June wish she had stuck with the original simple trim.

"Scared for your baby, cuz of the scorpions?" Kim asked, after giving another pointer to the young Myong, which also went ignored.

"Yeah."

"Wait..."

Kim walked away to the back room. June could hear another discussion in Korean take place. While Kim was away, June watched as Myong comtinued on in slow motion. Trying to see the back in the mirror, she was hopeful. Even if it wasn't being done in a top salon that Amy would patronize, it would be enough to perk up her appearance, and her attitude. Otherwise, not much had changed since the earlier trim.

Then Myong left her alone, also going to the back room. She returned with a pink reminder slip in her hand and gave it to June. She pointed with a polished nail at the writing.

"My friend, she married a hapa Hawaiian boy. His granny is Auntie Haunani." She said it as though it had a special meaning. "Maybe you can meet with her about your baby."

"Oh? I've met someone named Auntie Haunani. I wonder if it's the same one?"

"Old Hawaiian lady in Paia. People say she know all the old legends, what to do with pregnant ladies."

"I see." June looked at the name and phone number on the paper while Myong went back to work. "Where's Paia?"

"Go past the airport on the main highway. Not too far. But call her first. Tell her you are friend of Myong. She'll know it." June watched Myong intently as she worked with the last of her hair that framed her face. "But go with empty tummy. She feed you a lot. Aunties on this island no like skinny pregnant ladies."

"It has to be the same lady," June said, more to herself. She had met a woman named Haunani, a relative of her first patient, several months before when she first moved to the island. At that time, the old woman had guessed June was pregnant, even before she was showing. Or maybe knew was a better word than guess. She had also tried overfeeding June then.

Kim came out and smiled at June, giving her a thumbs up.

"Thanks," June said, holding the slip of paper up.

"What about the bangs?" Myong combed some hair across June's forehead as an example. "Want them shorter?"

Ever since her childhood when they were forced on her with every haircut, June had never liked bangs on herself, and had mostly avoided them. She could like them on other women, even her twin sister Amy, but they just didn't work for her. For that reason, she was trying to grow them out. She tried to visualize them on her face anyway.

"I don't know…"

"Keep them long, so can grow out quick if you don't like?"

She tried one last time to visualize them. "Better leave them alone for now."

While Kim sat in her chair with her magazine, Myong put the finishing touches on June's new style. Nothing much had changed since the trim the girl had done earlier, fine with June. It seemed to be more of a training session than anything else. At least she got a few questions answered about scorpions and comets. Without the conversation, Myong dried quickly, getting a little lift in it. It wasn't long before she was finished with the simple but pretty style.

At the end, June overpaid the stylist handsomely, not just for the service, but for the phone number and the use of the bathroom. What had started out as begging to use the bathroom turned into two hours of doting over a simple trim and some information.

While she took a few business cards, someone came in the door. To her surprise, it was Marilyn, from her earlier appointment at the Goddess Center, or whatever it was called, June couldn't remember exactly. What she did recall was the lie she'd told the woman about going to the other birth angel right after her earlier appointment.

Caught in her lie, and being stared at by Marilyn, June forced her prettiest smile.

"I thought you were going to see Katrina today?"

"Um, yes," June said. She needed to use her fake accent. "Sudden change in plans. I'm going to see her tomorrow."

"Katrina doesn't work on Sundays, except for wondrous births."

"Oh, tomorrow is Sunday?" June asked, playing innocent again. She noticed Myong watching the two of them closely. "I better call back and check."

Kim barked at Myong in Korean, drawing the girl away. While she put Marilyn in the chair June had just left, Kim took June outside to talk.

"How you know her?"

"Oh, I just met he a while ago."

"Not gonna be your doctor, yeah?"

"I…" June noticed Myong get to work on Marilyn, using electric clippers. "I doubt it."

Kim tossed her head in the direction of the salon. "That one, bad news. No one likes her. Stay away from her."

"That's what I was thinking, also."

With one last glance, Myong was making short order of Marilyn's hair, buzzing it close to her scalp. She would be finished soon, so June decided to get some distance between her and Marilyn, and waved goodbye to Kim.

"Hey, just stay away from that lady," Kim admonished as June retreated down the sidewalk.

***

The library wasn't far away, another place slightly air-conditioned and with a restroom. It would give her the chance to sit quietly and digest what she'd just heard from the stylists, and to research a few ideas. After more than a decade of working as a model in the past, one thing June knew was that stylists were notorious for passing gossip, but weren't necessarily dedicated to the truth.

Speed-reading articles in science journals refreshed her knowledge about scorpions, the power of the venom in their stings, and how very few in the world had lethal venom. Only the frailest of people and infants with undeveloped immune systems died from most stings, and often needed to be stung by several of the creatures at once to get a lethal dose. She also found no indications of studies having been done on the effects on fetuses when pregnant women were stung, if the venom even crossed the placental barrier between mother and fetus.

She returned the reference materials to the librarian and left, going back out into the humid afternoon.

"That brought up more questions than it answered," she muttered as she walked in the opposite direction of both the salon and Marilyn's Pandora's Box of Weirdness. She had to pass a coffee shop, the scent of coffee drifting out the door like an advertisement. Forcing herself to not go in, she continued on. Along with wine, she'd given up on caffeine when she learned she was pregnant, and wasn't sure which she would go back to first when the time came.

Further up the street, June sat on a bench in the shade. She wasn't sure if she still had the business card she was given during a police investigation in which she was witness. Digging through her pocketbook, she found the dog-eared card for a MPD detective. She kept her fingers crossed as she dialed his number.

"Detective Atkins? This is June Kato, of West Maui Medical Center. Do you by any chance remember me?"

He did and they exchanged a few pleasantries.

"What's on your mind, Doctor? From the standpoint of the police department, the Baxter case is wrapped up, neat and tidy. Anybody you have to worry about is in prison."

"It's something else, something you might be interested in hearing. Have you been following the news stories about these scorpion stings and deaths lately on Maui?"

"I have and it's a shame for those women. But that's more of a medical matter and not something for the police."

"The thing is, I think there's more to it than just simple stings. Five women, all with very similar backgrounds, all dying within days or weeks of each other under very similar circumstances is highly unusual from a medical standpoint."

"Explain to me what you're thinking," he said.

June explained her suspicions, how terribly unlikely it was to have such similarities, and how it went far beyond coincidence for those women to have died in very similar ways—and so close together.

"Doctor, from the point of view of the police and the District Attorney, there needs to be some sense of wrong-doing before anything can be investigated as a potential crime. Do you suspect malfeasance on the behalf of the condos in which those women lived?"

"Even though that's something consistent with each of them, no. Something else that's even more consistent are these so-called birth angels. I know for a fact that at least two of the victims have gone to them."

She had to explain the term 'birth angel' to the detective, her suspicions about them being related to the scorpion deaths, and how West Maui Med was involved.

"How do you know two of them have been to see these birth angels?" he asked. "Have they been patients of yours? Did they report something that happened to them?"

That's where June was stuck. "Well, no. One is a patient in the ICU right now and the other has passed away."

"The one in the ICU reported a birth angel used a scorpion in her treatment?"

"No. The last I saw, she was still unconscious, unable to speak. I only learned about it from the nurse taking care of her, who heard about it from the Emergency Room workers."

"And the dead woman?" he asked.

"From the newspaper."

"Doctor Kato, your information, while possibly being reliable, is second or third hand at best. To the police, that isn't much better than idle gossip heard in the produce department of the supermarket."

June felt deflated. "There's no way you can look into it?"

"Give me evidence of wrong-doing on someone's part. Give me evidence of anything that might indicate the deaths have been anything other than naturally occurring. I can't arrest scorpions, Doctor."

June had heard enough from him and ended their conversation with insincere gratitude. The scent of coffee drifted to her from the shop partway down the block. Hoping it was somewhat air-conditioned, she went there. Inside, she ordered a fruit drink, and relied on the scent of coffee as second-hand caffeination to perk her up. While she waited, she saw Marilyn Scanlon pass down the sidewalk just outside the shop windows, her newly shorn head illuminated by the sun. Turning and ducking behind a corner, she hid as best she could from the strange woman. Getting her drink, she sat at a table toward the back away from the windows.

"Just being dark in here is relaxing," she muttered, resting her head back against the seat cushion. She opened her ideas when something occurred to her. "Wait."

She dug through the articles she'd had printed at the library.

"They're nocturnal. Scorpions come out at night to hunt for food, preferring to stay in shelters, holes, cracks, places where they won't be exposed during the daytime. They prefer to remain in places where insect life is plentiful. They eat mice, large insects, other arachnids, even rats." She referred to some other notes she'd made after reading news articles. "Each of the women have been stung during the daytime, indoors, and in modern condos. Maybe being pregnant doesn't have anything to do with it, and it really is a coincidence? Maybe, just maybe, they spent most of their time at home, in condos, because they were pregnant, and were simply victims of scorpions that had somehow found their way into their units?"

June borrowed a phone book from the barista. Getting one last whiff of coffee, she gave in.

"Can I get an iced decaf, please? And if a little caffeinated coffee happens to splash intot he cup, it wouldn't be a bad thing."

"Gotcha," the barista said, smiling.

June paid and took her beloved elixir to her table, sipping as she went.

"Okay, public health department." Dialing her phone, she called the public information and access extension. Following the menu, she finally got a live person on the line. Once again, she had to be careful how she framed her language. "Yes, hi. I'm a physician at West Maui Medical Center and I've been following the crisis of scorpions stings and pregnant women on Maui lately. Are there any updates?"

"Crisis? Updates? What crisis?"

"Several women have died as the result of scorpion stings in the last few weeks. Days, really."

"You mean you're concerned about what has been reported in the news lately?" the woman asked.

"Exactly. Are there updates on the causes or how the community can protect themselves?"

"Let me assure you, Miss, that there is no crisis. Not as far as public health officials are concerned."

"How can it not be?" June asked. "Several women have died, and two more are in the hospital. It isn't unusual to you that single pregnant women all living in a specific part of the island have been stung, and have died as a result?"

"Let me explain, Miss, that what they've been reporting on the television news isn't entirely correct. In fact, it has been rather inflammatory, with no empirical basis to their claims whatsoever," the woman said officiously. "During cane harvest times, there's always an uptick in spider bites and scorpion stings. It's one of the many hazards of working in agriculture. The number of sting victims this year is little different from any other year. Only about fifty percent higher."

"Maybe you haven't noticed, but much of the cane fields have gone fallow, with very little harvesting being done these days. The other problem with your argument is that none of the sting patients have been agricultural workers. They've all been indoors, during the daytime, and pregnant. How do you account for that?" June demanded.

"In agricultural populations, pregnant women have been working in the fields for centuries. You know the old joke of how a woman working in a rice paddy gives birth, cuts the cord by biting through it, and goes back to work while holding the baby under one arm?"

June swore to herself. "Pardon me?"

"Surely you know what I mean."

"Yes, I think I do. By the way, what was your name again?"

"Clara Cayne."

"Your job title?" June asked.

"I'm a senior field researcher."

"Not for long. Have a nice day."

As far as June could tell, public health officials were monitoring the problem because of what was being reported in the news, but not because they felt there was a risk to the people of Maui. She got no further with them than she did with the police detective.

After sipping some of her cold coffee, and not knowing what else to do, she dialed Auntie Haunani's number. It had to be the same woman she had met eight months earlier, and she hoped she would be remembered by the elderly woman.

Her call to the Hawaiian lady rang several times, and just as she was rethinking the wisdom of asking even more questions about scorpions and folklore, her call was answered.

"Hello?" the accent was heavy, and the voice deep, but female.

"Yes, hello. My name is June Kato and I was given your phone number by a mutual friend. I heard you might be able to help me."

She was suddenly reversing direction on wanting to meet with the old Hawaiian woman. There had been some minor trouble the first time they met and didn't want to start more. If she really wanted to know about scorpions, she could just as easily keep reading about them. No reason to bother old ladies over trivial things.

"You that hapai doctor lady that help Kekoa?" the old lady asked.

"I am. I see Kekoa around the hospital occasionally." Kekoa was June's first patient on the island when June first moved there. Part of a large Hawaiian family on the island, Kekoa worked as a lab tech at the hospital. June had met Haunani back then, and the old lady not only remembered her name, she remembered June was pregnant. "I was hoping to talk with you about something that's been troubling me lately."

There was an impatient sigh. "About the scorpions."

June was surprised the lady knew. "Yes. I'm sorry, maybe I shouldn't have bothered you with something so trivial."

"You want protect keiki from perish?" the woman asked, using the local terminology for child.

"Yes, that's right. You see…"

"Already know you hapai. Should be any day now, yeah?"

"Two weeks."

"Maybe baby impatient. When you want come?"

June looked at her watch again, and tried to figure what time the sun would set. The last thing she wanted to do was drive around unfamiliar streets in the dark, just to make the drive home along a stretch of road she knew was accident prone. She was frustrated by her parents being overly protective of her while she was pregnant, so much so it felt like she was a teenager again. Just being out all day without checking in with them was going to cause enough trouble; was she willing to stir up even more?

"I could come now?"

"Today gone pau. Come for kau kau…for lunch tomorrow. You know come?"

It sounded like English, but June could barely understand the lady. "Um, no, I don't have your address."

There was no formal address, but June got driving directions to a house somewhere, she wasn't quite sure, she'd have to look on a map later. All she knew was that Haunani lived on the 'other side', whatever that meant.

"Can I bring something?" June asked.

"Pohaku from behind house."

"Pardon?" June wondered if it was some sort of wildflower.

"Not pardon, pohaku. A stone," the woman said impatiently. "It will rain before sunrise. Get one then, from big rock pile up the hill behind house. You know it?"

There was indeed a rocky outcropping of sorts, a giant pile of rough *a'a* type of lava that had been pushed there by bulldozers grading the slope for new construction. She had her suspicions that's exactly where the scorpions were coming from before invading her house.

"Yes. It'll rain tomorrow?"

"Rain like heck until the sun comes up. Make'm tutu drive you."

"Tutu?" June asked to a dead line. She looked at the phone, and sure enough, the call had ended.

Having wasted enough time, she gave up on her little expedition to town and went back to the car. As soon as she had the engine turned on, she ramped the A/C up to the top.

It took only a few minutes to get out of old Wailuku town and on the highway around to West Maui and home.

"So, tonight it's going to rain, and I'm supposed to go out before sunrise and get a rock. Evidently any rock, just from the rock pile up the hill. And I'm supposed to have Tutu drive me to her house, whoever that might be. And I need to find Auntie Haunani's house out in some old sugar cane field, but with no address. Just so I can learn about scorpions? What am I getting into?" June took a long, deep breath. "There's something screwy about this scorpion stuff."

The sun was getting low, and slanted in through the windshield, hitting her eyes after she passed through the short highway tunnel. After following curves on the coastline road, the sun was shining on her face. She turned off the A/C and rolled the window down, sticking her arm out the window to catch the warm breeze. She kept to the highway, passing through Lahaina Town to Ka'anapali. The closer she got to home, the slower she drove.

She didn't care the fruit juice and iced coffee were colliding with her bladder, that the moment was that enjoyable.

June hadn't had any real fights with her parents since they moved in, only minor spats that were quickly forgotten, or deemed too unimportant to carry on. She appreciated her parent's concern, but it was often stifling. She wasn't an invalid, even if she was moving more slowly with each passing week of pregnancy. But she wondered if one was coming that evening because she'd been out all day.

She had one more place to go, and that was to make rounds on her patients at the hospital. That gave her one more hour of time away from home, and a clean bathroom to visit.

Her mother was at the stove when she went in the house.

"Is Rodney still here?" she asked right off. If Rodney was already gone, she may as well face the beast.

"Left about an hour ago." Mabel kept her eyes on what she was cooking on the stove. "You were gone all day. We were worried."

"I know. I just wanted some time alone."

"You should've called."

"Yeah, I should've done a lot of things." Most of the day had been dead ends, or ends that led to more new questions than what she'd had answered. Even the lift in her new hairstyle wasn't holding up in the humidity.

"What happened to you?" her father asked when he walked into the kitchen.

"Spent the afternoon in town, okay? I'm old enough."

"You never called. Your mom needed the car for errands."

"The pickup was available."

June pushed past him to go to her bedroom. It was becoming her hideout, a place for respite. Pulling off most of her clothes, she turned on the fan and stood before it, trying to recoup the sense of A/C she felt in the car.

There was a knock at the door. "Yes?"

"Can we talk?" her father asked.

She pulled on a layer of clothes, sitting on the bed with the fan blowing directly at her. "Okay."

"I heard you were getting a massage and coming home right after," he said quietly.

"I said I was going to town for a massage. I don't remember anything about timelines or curfews."

"What took so long?"

"Oh, looking for bathrooms, getting a haircut, reading in the library. Nothing terribly strenuous." She grinned at him. "Not as strenuous as being interrogated about it, anyway."

"That took several hours?"

She didn't want to try and explain about the oddball session with Marilyn, so she changed the subject. "After rounds at the hospital tomorrow, I have someplace to go. Can you or Mom take me?"

"Back to town? For what?"

"There's a lady I know, and I have an appointment to meet with her."

"Appointment? About the baby?" he asked.

"Sort of. She might have some information about all these scorpions and how we might be able to keep them out of the house."

"They're scorpions. We can just sweep them out the door."

"You also said you were going to make a scorpion repeller for the back door, but so far, nada."

He leaned against the doorframe. "I'm still working on it."

"Maybe you haven't been paying attention, Dad. Several pregnant women on the island have died in the last few weeks, all of them suffering scorpions stings just before their deaths. Plus, two more are in the ICU trying to recover from stings. I was just there and saw them with my own eyes. I don't want the same thing for me, okay?"

"Just relax, June. You're too uptight."

"Don't you dare tell me I'm uptight! Pregnant woman are dying from scorpion stings, I'm pregnant, and I'm living in Scorpion Central, Dad!"

He sat on the bed, keeping a safe gap between them. "Tell me what you know about the scorpion stings."

"I've been doing some reading about venom crossing the placental barrier, and few studies have been done. Results have been inconclusive if insect venoms can cross from the mother's bloodstream into that of the fetus. Maybe you can just sweep the problem out the door but I'm pretty dang nervous about it."

"I didn't know it was that serious."

"I could lose the baby if I was stung. Scorpions, spiders, even those big, ugly centipedes have found their way into the house. I have to inspect my bed, all my clothes before getting dressed, the floor when I go to the bathroom eighty-seven stupid times every night. And once the baby comes, who's going to stand guard cribside? You?"

"Who is this lady you're going to see tomorrow?" he asked.

"An old Hawaiian lady I met a while back, before you and Mom moved in." She wasn't sure how well he'd accept the idea she was going to a kahuna for help. "She's a relative of one of my patients and helped a lot with his recovery. I talked to her today and she said she has some ideas that might help."

"How long will you be gone?" he asked.

"Maybe most of the day. She lives on the other side of the island somewhere. It might not be easy to find. That's why I want someone else to drive while I watch the map. Maybe Mom should take me. That'll let you work on the addition. How's that coming, anyway?"

"Rodney made good progress on the mudding."

"Yeah, I noticed him working by himself today. You need to remember, he's here on vacation, and not as your employee. He's supposed to be having a good time, which means you better be paying him well."

"He said he'd take minimum wage."

"What? Double that! No, triple it. And it's coming out of your pocket. Hiring him was your big idea, as was this addition, and all I heard before you started as that it would take a few weeks. Well, it's been several months and is costing me a heck of a lot more than your estimates. Now you have a kid spending his vacation doing your work, and you're paying him only minimum wage? Triple it, give him two meals a day, and a bonus at the end. In fact, he has the day off tomorrow. You're taking him to church in town and then sightseeing."

"Which church?"

"I don't know. All I know is he likes going to church on Sundays. I doubt he even cares which denomination. Just find a nice one and take him, buy him lunch, take him to the movies, or take a lap around the island. Just make sure he has some fun."

They were called to the dinner table by her mother.

"Your mom bought mint chip ice cream. Make sure you eat some tonight after dinner, okay?"

"What brand?"

"Local Maui dairy."

"Does it have gelatin in it?"

"I don't know."

"You can have mine."

***

After dinner, she called Henry, her first friend on the island. She got the directions to Auntie Haunani's house from her clutch.

"Remember we met Auntie Haunani last year? I'm supposed to meet her tomorrow about something. The problem is, she doesn't really have an address. She lives out in some old sugar cane field."

"There are still a lot of Hawaiians and Filipinos who live in those old houses. Same kind of house you live in. Did she give directions?"

"Near some place named Paia. Evidently, there's a paved road that goes up from the town, and a dirt road branches off it that goes to her house. That's all she told me."

"Not many roads around there. Those old dirt roads are called cane haul roads. Probably not too many houses along there. Every now and then, a developer comes along and buys up giant chunks of land like that and puts in a new subdivision. It's really too bad."

"Less history, more directions, Henry."

"There won't be many roads. Just follow the first one you get to until you see a house. Otherwise, there's no way of knowing where to go."

"Am I supposed to bring anything with me? A salad or some fruit for her?" June read her note again. "She told me to find a rock and bring that."

"A rock?"

"Yeah. She said to get a rock from near my house in the dark and bring that. To me, that sounds a little whacky. Is this some Hawaiian thing? To bring rocks?"

He laughed. "Who knows? You're dealing with a kahuna now, June. You better expect the unexpected! But why are you going to see Auntie Haunani?"

She didn't want to bring up her worries about the scorpions. But there was even more than that. Recently she had grown more worried about her pregnancy, the baby, and even though her OB had told her everything was fine except her low weight, June couldn't settle her nerves. "Oh, these stupid scorpions, my pregnancy, some other things. I guess I've begun obsessing over all these stories in the newspaper about scorpion stings and pregnant women. That's why I'm going to see Haunani."

"I can understand why."

"Do you know if any more women have been brought to the hospital with stings?"

"Not that I've heard, but I'll ask around."

"What's a tutu?" she asked. "I'm supposed to bring Tutu with me."

"Same as calling someone granny or grandpa. Probably your mom in this case. Make sure you take the truck. That big car your dad bought looks nice but won't get far on cane haul roads."

"Probably another wild goose chase on Maui. They would be more fun if I wasn't a hundred years pregnant and a walking sweat factory."

"Yeah, have fun with that."

Chapter Three

June lay on her bed, her cell phone in front her, tapping a fingernail to scroll through numbers, tears running unabated down her face. Along with obsessing over invasive bugs and spending her days looking for bathrooms, she had a short cry each evening, never really sure why. The same as always, she stopped at the one number that was best. She sent a text message.

Busy?

Getting the girls into bed.

Those few simple words from Amy brought a tiny smile to June's face.

Can we talk later?

Call Mick

June didn't want to talk to Mick, Amy's husband, and June's boyfriend from the distant past. The last time they actually talked was several months before, and that hadn't ended so well. It was the day of Amy's wedding, and on her prompting, June had to face the elephant in the room. Even though it had been years since June and Mick had been together as a couple, they had never officially broken up, at least in Amy's eyes. After being arm-twisted into the odd request, June complied. It hadn't been pretty, but that was life. Not a single word had passed between her and Mick since. Now, he was in fact, the last person she wanted to talk to.

No.

There was a pause, June figuring the girls were getting a story read to them or a scolding for being too busy in bed.

Just as she was wiping her face with the bed sheet, her phone rang with a call. She looked at the number through wet eyes.

"Come on, not you." She sighed and picked up the phone to answer. "Hey Mick. What's up?"

"How's the pregnant lady?"

"Nervous wreck. Totally neurotic. Can't stop crying. Haven't slept in a month. Don't eat much. Not earning a living. My parents run my life. And poisonous bugs are trying to kill my baby. Other than that, fantastic."

It poured out, as fast as the new surge of tears from her eyes.

"That's just stuff. But how are you, Babe?" he asked, using her lifelong nickname. In fact, only he and Amy were allowed to call June that. And right then, it was the most reassuring thing she could've heard, for her lifelong friend to call her Babe again. He really was her friend and she couldn't be mad at him any longer.

"That's what's going on right now."

"Yeah, that's what's going on. But it's not you. I want to know how you are."

"Me?" she asked again.

"Yeah, you. What's going on inside June Kato? What are the nerves all about?"

"I just told you a minute ago…my parents, scorpions, and big ugly centipedes, the baby."

"Come on. You've dealt with your parents all your life. And you've had bigger enemies than bugs."

June continued drying her face. "I don't know how to have a baby, Mick. I don't know what I'm doing. I got a tiny little person inside me and I know I'm going screw it up."

"Have you ever screwed up anything? Seriously malfunctioned at anything in your life?"

"Like, yeah!" she said sarcastically.

"You've made mistakes along the way. But nothing you couldn't resolve. So have the rest of us." When he paused, she didn't know what to say back. He was right about that though, that she had survived some tough spots. She might've come away shaken a bit, but came away. "You know what your problem is?"

"Tell me, Oh Great Wizard of Oz!" she said. Everybody else was full of advice for her. She may as well get it from him also.

"Your problem is you've always been the best at everything you do. Being at the top isn't good enough for you. Everything has to be perfect. And now your pregnancy has to be perfect, and you'll have to be a perfect mother. But guess what? You won't be. The baby might not have the ideal birth weight, or be a whole week behind in some insignificant development milestone, or will have a scratch on its hand. Then you'll beat yourself up for being a rotten mother because you haven't achieved the ideal and made it even better."

Nothing could piss June off faster than being told the truth. He gave her nothing she could argue about.

She rolled onto her back, but when the baby kicked, she went back to her side.

"I'm just worried," she said with a sigh.

"I know. The rest of us are also. That's why your folks are there, nagging you about every little thing. You've had problems before, about the miscarriage a long time, and everybody just wants you to be okay."

Only Amy had known about the ancient miscarriage, promised to keep it secret, but somehow the rest of the family now knew.

"You know about that?"

"You think your family doesn't talk to each other? Amy told us when we found out you were pregnant. That's why your mom and dad moved in with you. Even if you were still back in LA, they probably would've moved in."

"Yep, probably." June wondered if she should ask the next question, and had a good idea of Mick's answer. "Any advice?"

"Suck it up. And don't worry about being a good mother. You already are. Here's Amy."

"How's it goin'?" Amy asked. "Staying hydrated?"

Her tears had stopped, but June knew what Amy meant. "Not lately. How often do you and Mom talk, anyway?"

"Every time you have one of your nervous breakdowns, which is about three times a day lately."

"Just about."

"Are you eating?"

"The baby is. I get a few leftovers. My belly is so big now and I'm dropping already. I think someone's inflating a blimp in there."

"Yeah, but two weeks from now, you're gonna have the prettiest little baby ever born, right there in your arms."

"This ends someday?"

"Believe it or not, it does. And six months later, you'll want to do it all over again." It was quiet in the call behind Amy's voice for a change, and June knew she had her undivided attention for a while. "Mom said you're still going to work."

Somehow, it was safe now, as though Amy was with her in the room instead of across the ocean. "It's not much. And I need the money. That new addition on the back of the house is taking longer than what I was promised, and costing a lot more than what Dad promised."

"Don't worry about the room. It keeps him occupied. What are they doing tomorrow?"

"After badgering me to eat more at breakfast, he's taking Rodney out for the day. Then Mom and I have some errands to do."

"See? Life's good, if you arrange it that way. But don't get too far from the hospital. You're running out of time, Babe. Be smart about the next couple of weeks."

"Yeah. But hey. I go see a Hawaiian kahuna tomorrow."

"For?" Amy asked.

"She has ideas on how to keep the bugs out of the house."

"Get an exterminator and be done with it. But how did you find a bug kahuna?"

"Met her a while back. Long story."

June told her sister the long story of Kekoa and Auntie Haunani, and the old Hawaiian spirit traditions she'd learned a few months before. It had been an strange but brief chapter in her life, but in the end, it all turned out fine.

"Like I just told you, be smart about the next couple of weeks."

There was a tap at June's door.

"Yeah?" June called out.

"Can I come in?" her mom asked from out in the hall.

"On the phone!" she called out. "It's Mom," June said to Amy. "She hasn't lectured me in at least an hour. I better go."

"Yes, time for your evening browbeating. I remember those well when I was preggie with the twins." Amy switched her voice to a higher pitched comical tone. *"You're not eating enough...you'll just get sick...you have babies coming...you work too much...you need to rest more."*

"Ha! I got them all memorized."

"Babe, I still hear them in my sleep! But she means well, and she's right. You need to take care. And eat a snack before going to bed."

June ended the call, took a picture of her belly, and sent it. She tossed the phone down on the bed and went to the bathroom. By the time she was back, a text was waiting for her.

I want another!

There was another knock at the door, the way her mother knocks. June just didn't want to climb off the bed to let her in. "What, Mom?"

Mabel went in and sat on the edge of the bed, near where June had her head on a pillow. She stroked her hand over June's back, the same as whenever one of them was sick in bed as a kid.

"Everything okay?"

"Tired of peeing all the time."

"Can I help?"

"Lend me your bladder for a few days." Her mother's gentle touch felt good right then. "Just talked to Amy…and Mick. They talked me down again."

"You don't have do this all alone, Dear. Married to Jack, then suddenly single, having a baby, living in a new town, and getting a new job, all at the same time is pretty tough. The rest of us want to help."

"I know. It's just…"

"You don't know how to ask for help."

"Yeah," June mumbled quietly, snuggling her pillow in closer.

"What can Dad and I do tomorrow?" her mother asked.

An olive branch was being extended. June was getting control back.

"Dad already has his assignment for tomorrow. Whether he does it or not, I don't care. As long as he's not in my gun sights." June started to push up, but lay back down again. "Get my clutch." She poked through it, getting out the directions for Haunani's house. "See if you can find this place on a map. That's our errand."

"Where'd you go today?" Mabel asked quietly, while looking at the slip.

"There's a lady in town, like a doula, but pretty weird."

"And you went to see her? What's wrong with your OB, with Doctor Gill?"

"Nothing is wrong with her. I'm still scheduled for two weeks from now. But this lady had something to do with one of the women that are in the hospital right now."

"The latest one with the scorpion sting, the one at your hospital?"

"Yeah. I saw her in the ICU yesterday. Something doesn't seem right about all these pregnant woman dying of scorpion stings. There's a second one in the hospital now."

"Are the police looking into it?" he mother asked.

"Not that I'm aware of. Nobody else thinks there's anything suspicious about it but me."

"Probably because you're pregnant, and a little suspicious of everything. But why did yo go see her if you think she's nutty?"

"I was just curious if she had anything to do with those women."

"You didn't see the news today? Another lady died."

June lifted her head to look her mother in the eyes. "Really?"

"It's sad. Too many pregnant women that have died from scorpion stings. And they said on the news there's another lady in that other hospital in town."

June struggled to sit up, trying in vain to pull her shirt down over her belly.

"That's too many for other reasons, Mom. That many pregnant women dying from scorpion stings in one place in short succession? And apparently all of them from respiratory collapse due to anaphylactic shock? One is understandable. Two, maybe. But not five or six. There shouldn't be that many nationwide in a year, let alone on a small island in such a short time."

June pushed up from the bed and began to waddle away.

"Where are you going?" her mother asked.

"Where else?"

"Come out to the kitchen when you're done. There's still leftover potatoes."

June reheated a plate of buttery potatoes. Waiting for her at the table were both her parents. She pulled her chair out and set it sideways to the table. She stabbed a piece of potato and took a bite, chewing slowly.

"June..."

"Dad, I'm sorry. I've been taking so much out on you guys lately, and I don't mean it. I'm just so..."

"We came here to make things easier for you, and to see the baby. But maybe we're just in the way?" her dad asked.

"No, you're not in the way. I've been in my own way. I appreciate all the work you guys do, on the new room, and taking care of everything. You have no idea how great it is to have you here, really."

"At least you're eating more," he father said. "I guess I finally found something you'll eat."

"You've gained since last week. I can see it in your face," her mother said.

"There's something I can be proud of. My face is catching up with my butt."

"Not much choice, Dear. Just keep feeding the baby." There was a pause when June finished her potatoes and tried to get up to take the plate to the sink. It ended up not worth the effort. "Talk to Jack lately?"

"A few days ago. I should call him."

"Is he excited?"

"He says he is. He says he's still dedicated to being involved in the baby's life, at least as much as he can be…" June sighed. "…from the White House."

"I hope he comes through, at least with money for a good education," her father said.

"I can't believe I'm going to give birth to a President's kid. How silly is that? Five thousand miles apart, we were married but not really, and whoever this is inside of me is going to grow up never knowing they deserve Secret Service protection. And here I am trying to keep from being stung by poisonous bugs. Can my life get any more absurd?"

***

June listened to her father snore from the other bedroom. She heard the toilet flush, which meant her mother wasn't sleeping through the snoring either. She grabbed her phone from the nightstand and tapped. There were six time zones between her and the baby's father, which meant he would be sitting at a desk someplace.

"Hi, Jack. Busy?"

"Not in the Situation Room, but that doesn't mean much lately. What's up?"

"I read about that incident in Gaza a while back, and the deal you made to prevent it from happening again. I assume at least some of what the media reported was accurate?"

"Mostly. Except now I'm known as the guy who brokers deals with terrorists. I'm still not so sure which side of the deal was more terroristic, which is something that can't be leaked to the news media, June."

"If there isn't death and bloodshed in the streets, does it really matter who the good guys are?"

"Anymore, not really. Enough of my dramas. How is the baby? Been to the OB lately? Two more weeks, right?"

"My OB is happy except I'm still a little underweight. The baby's heart pounds like an athlete's and has the kick of an NFL placekicker. According to the latest ultrasound, the kid is going to be tall, taking after you."

"How are you?"

"Okay. Like I said, still a little tired."

"Come on, June. That's not what I meant."

"A little scared sometimes. You're not abandoning our kid, right?"

He gave his usual mild scolding, for the same question she always asked on their calls. "We've discussed this a thousand times. I can't leave the White House and you're unwilling to move here. In three years, we can be together. Where, I have no idea. You seem dedicated to living and raising the kid there, so I need to start considering a solution that includes that."

"More like seven years, isn't it?" she asked, thinking of a second term in office.

"Probably, depending on the ideas of voters. But I don't have to run again."

"You're doing America a lot of good, Jack. That's something both of us need to think about when re-election time comes again."

"June, you're willing to make that sacrifice?"

"It's not like I'm going to war, Jack. I also won't be the first mother in America to raise a kid by herself." June scolded herself. "Sorry, I didn't mean it to sound that way."

"But you would be," he said. "There's no way of knowing right now if I'll win an re-election bid, not even in the primaries."

"You won last time by a seventy percent landslide. You even have the terrorist vote for the next election." She dried a wet eye with her bed sheet. "Sorry, that also was unnecessary."

"Better than what one of the networks is saying about me today."

"Oh? More trouble?"

"Wait till morning to watch the news."

"Should I worry?" she asked.

"I'm not. By the end of the month, it'll turn out to be nothing. But in the next couple of weeks, life in the White House won't be so jolly."

"I saw the deposit in the baby's trust fund. That wasn't necessary. You've already put twice as much in there as what you promised."

"I'm not trying to buy your love or that of the baby. I just want to be sure Jack Junior has the money to pay for a good education when the time comes."

She smiled. "Why Jack Junior? Why not June Junior?" she asked.

"Does the world really need another June Kato?"

"Ha! I suppose not. But just so you know, no one else knows about the trust fund, not my parents or Amy, no one. If something should happen to me, you'll have to…"

"Happen to you? What are you talking about? That's a little gloomy, even for you."

"Oh, there seems to be a plague of poisonous beasts in West Maui these days, and my house is their club meeting place." She explained about the scorpions, and the deaths of several pregnant women, and how those deaths were related somehow to the scorpions in the area. "We sweep one or two out the door everyday."

"Whatever you do, don't spray chemicals. Not good for the baby."

"I'm doing my best to not kill any of them, but I'm losing my patience."

"You mean you'd actually resort to killing something?" he asked.

"No, but I might not notice if my dad does. If it gets any worse, I might need to have you send in the Marines again."

"How's the house holding up?"

As a welcome gift, Jack Melendez had ordered a squad of Marines to go to Maui and remodel her old house into something livable when June first moved there. It was also something of a wedding gift. Only days before they had married in a hastily arranged ceremony on the Oval Office, with the promise of a true wedding once he was out of office. June had hated the idea of playing First Lady, giving up on her medical career to hold tea receptions in the Rose Garden. That was before either of them knew she was pregnant. The ceremony had been so hasty that the minister who performed the rites was indeed not licensed in

Washington DC, meaning the wedding hadn't been legal, leaving June truly a single mother. As it stood now, the only people who knew of the ceremony were the few who witnessed it, her parents, and Amy. The only ones who knew of the father's identity were her closest family and Divya, her OB. It wasn't as if anyone, including Jack, was ashamed of him being the father; it was the scandal for him that would arise if the world knew. There would be no way the situation could be explained publically so anyone could come out looking decent. But it meant June would raise a child fathered by a sitting President as a single woman, at least until they could find a time and place to marry.

"It's fine. Dad's almost done with the addition. He has some help. Rodney, if you remember him? He and his sister are visiting right now."

"June, I have to go. Call me soon, or at least when labor starts."

"Just one quick request, Jack. Can you find a staffer with time of their hands to find out if a comet is headed toward Maui's sky?"

With that, she was left alone. Unable to sleep, she grabbed the phone book and flipped through several sections, looking for government offices.

She jotted notes on a pad of paper, with the address and hours of the county coroner's office. There was only one morgue on the island, located in the basement of the larger hospital in town. Relying on her credentials as a practicing doctor on the island, June made the plan to ask a few questions of the coroner. She wouldn't have time during the week, unless she took off from work early, so she made the tentative plan to go in the afternoon, after her visit with the Hawaiian kahuna.

Just as she was setting her phone aside, she heard the patter of rain on the metal roof, just like Haunani had predicted. The drumming got louder as the rain fell harder.

That's when she remembered she had to get the rock before dawn during the rain.

"A rock? Just any old rock?" she asked herself in the dark of night. "And does it have to be raining when I get it?"

Her father continued to snore, and she heard her mother's footsteps go down the hall past her door toward the kitchen. Some water ran in the kitchen sink, and there was the clank of the kettle on the stove. She would be making chamomile tea.

June didn't need to look at the clock to know the time. It was smack in the middle of the night, the time when any sane person would be deeply asleep. It was also time for another trip to the bathroom if she had any hope of getting sleep that night.

Thinking about the differences between Scanlon and Haunani, June felt a little embarrassed. While she had been condemning Scanlon for what she considered bizarre behavior with pebbles and an aura cleansing, she was looking forward to her visit with Haunani, the kahuna, and her history with rocks and leaves in spiritual practices. June thought again about collecting the rock at dawn, and the pebbles Marilyn had used in the parlor tricks or fortune telling or whatever it was that afternoon.

"What's with all the rock collecting on this island?" she said, returning to her room from the bathroom. "I shouldn't talk, since I've been going along with whatever they've told me. Ever since Marilyn did her trick with the pebbles and told me about the comet, all I've done is try to link that to scorpions. She even denied knowing any correlation between the two. But then I listen to a hairdresser for advice about bugs, and sign up for a session with a kahuna? Me thinks I'm the nutty one in the group."

Grabbing one of the articles she'd copied at the library that day, she read more about the pathology of scorpion stings to refresh her memory. It turned out that scorpions were not endemic to Hawaii, but were recent arrivals, most likely off ships in ports, coming in with fruits and vegetables, or out of shipping containers. They liked dusty terrain, living almost exclusively on the drier sides of each island. Most of the stings people suffered were from surprising the creature, working in cane fields and agriculture, and occasionally by children playing with them.

"Extremely rare that they are fatal, and no neurotoxins in the scorpions of the Hawaiian Islands," June read to herself. "Medical treatment is limited, often only requiring antibiotics and a tetanus shot to prevent infection."

She set the article aside.

"So, why all the deaths from anaphylaxis? A new strain of scorpion that has just come in off a boat, something more poisonous than the ones already here?" She looked at the notes she had started on a scratch pad of paper. "All five women were staying in condos, and here in the West Maui area. And they were all pregnant women, highly unlikely they were working in fields, or even pea patches. Most condos would frown on pea patches, right?" she asked herself in the dark.

Next, she looked at the death report data for the island, something she had found with the help of a librarian. There were none related to scorpions or spiders until these recent five deaths, only a single death related to a centipede bite on a child several months before.

"Great. Now I need to worry about giant man-eating centipedes also." She sighed and turned off the bedside lamp. "What kind of deathtrap is this island?"

June heard a chair scrape on the linoleum floor in the kitchen. Between her bladder and her mom sitting alone to drink her tea, she had enough incentive to struggle out of bed. She shone her flashlight around the floor, and seeing no bugs scurry away, she settled her feet down and shuffled off to the bathroom before going to the kitchen.

"Mom," she said when she got there. She poured hot water in a cup for herself.

"Did I wake you?"

June settled into a chair. "Bathroom. Usually the sound of rain puts me out. These days, it just encourages the inevitable."

The windows were open. The patter of rain splashing off the roof in sheets onto the hard ground outside was soothing to June. It cooled, even refreshed her somehow.

"Can I ask you a question?" June asked her mom. "Don't think of it because I'm a doctor asking, or any other way, just with an open mind."

She got the go-ahead.

"There've been five deaths on this island in the last few days, all from scorpion bites, all pregnant women, all relative newcomers here. Does that seem odd to you?"

"I don't know much about medicine."

"Well, not thinking about it like that, but just in general terms. Does it seem like a lot?" June asked again.

"I guess it does. It almost seems like an epidemic, with all of them so close together."

"It almost is. Five victims, in one general area, close together in occurrence, with similar causative agents. I think the population of the island is about a hundred thousand people, and for a population that size, five all at once could almost be considered an epidemic. Plus the other two that are in the hospital getting treatment. But the peculiarity doesn't stop there. All have been women, all have been recent arrivals, and all have been late term pregnant. And they've even been living in condos. Either there's been a massive population explosion of condo-dwelling scorpions on the island, or that's one heck of a coincidence."

"Is there anything else in medicine that's similar?" he mother asked.

"Well, I'm not an expert, but usually public health diseases and crises follow something of a pattern. An expert can follow the disease pattern backward to see where the epidemic started, and in that way they can fix the current problem by eliminating the risk, and reduce the chances for it happening again in the future. That's called epidemiology."

"I don't understand."

"One sick person, usually someone who doesn't realize they're sick, shows up in a community. They pass the disease on to someone else, then they pass it on to others, and so on. Finding what's common between them all and then tracing it backward is what leads to the original person. That person is known as 'patient zero'. Like when there's an outbreak of hepatitis. Public health officials interview everyone who got sick, see what places they ate at and dates that were in common, check the staffing for that restaurant for those dates, and bingo, they have their culprit, the person who doesn't wash their hands very well."

"What's that have to do with scorpions on Maui?" her mother asked.

"Nothing. That's just it. I bet if somebody from the public health department or even the police department looked into these deaths in that way, they'd find no single person or scorpion to trace to, no similarities..."

June stopped mid-sentence. What she'd just said made no sense at all. There was a public health crisis on the island, but there would be no patient zero to blame if the crisis was naturally to blame. The similarities were with the victims, not with the disease. There was no contagion or carrier. It wasn't one scorpion going around attacking women, it was a different bug each time. No one was passing a disease from one woman to the next. Women were being stung by scorpions, plain and simple, each a well-defined and separate event unto itself. It wasn't the fault of the scorpions; the fault lie with the women for being stung.

"This really doesn't make any sense at all," June said, sipping some of her mother's tea.

"Maybe the lady we see in the morning will know something?" Mabel asked.

"I hope so. I'm supposed to bring a pohaku, a rock, with me to the appointment."

"What kind?"

"I don't know. She seemed to know there was a big rock pile up the hill from us, and said to go up there before sunrise in the rain and get a rock. But I don't know why."

Her mother shrugged. "So, go get a rock."

"But I want to know why?"

"Maybe it's enough to just be obedient this time? Do as she said. Take your flashlight, go out in the rain, grab a rock, and come back. You can get a shower after that. If you like, we can go out for breakfast on the way to your kahuna friend." Mabel smiled a mischievous grin. "But it might be best to not say anything to you father about the rock. Seems like he's almost as superstitious as you."

"Can you come with me? I'd feel like a dope out there by myself looking for a rock in the dark and rain."

"Just come get me when you go. We can be silly together," her mother said. "How did you hear about this lady again?"

"Well, I met her earlier this year, when her nephew was a patient of mine in the hospital. She came in to see him, sort of the spiritual advisor for the family. Then when I was in the salon yesterday, one of the stylists gave me her name and phone number again. Evidently, this Haunani is much more well-known on the island than I ever thought."

"And she's okay?" Mabel asked. "What I mean is, she's not…"

"A head case?"

"Might be a better way of putting it, but yes."

"This whole island has a special way of doing things, Mom," June muttered, picking at a nail. "We're not in LA anymore."

June's father had quit snoring, so it was safe for them to go back to bed. From experience, June knew if they could get to sleep right away, she might be able to sleep through the next round of snoring.

June got more sleep. When she woke, it was still dark. Looking at the time, it was close enough to dawn to pull little rock-hunting caper. June left on her old T-shirt and shorts, since they were ripe from sweating all night. A little rainwater wasn't going to change that. She crept down the hall to her parent's room, flashing her light back and forth on scorpion patrol. She just needed to get her mom and go find a rock.

When she got outside their room, she didn't knock. There were warning signs in the sounds that came through the door, sounds she'd heard before, even as far back as childhood. She didn't want to interrupt what they were doing.

'Someone may as well have some fun in the house,' she thought, tiptoeing past their room.

When she got to the back door, she put on a hooded windbreaker used while gardening on rainy days. There was too much mud to walk through barefoot, so she grabbed her father's heavy-duty rubber boots to use. She shone the light down inside looking for critters, shook each one upside-down to knock any unpermitted residents out, and shoved her feet down into them.

Silently closing the door behind her, she went along the side of the house toward the back and continued through the pea patch garden, getting drenched in the storm. The boots were much too large for her bare feet, making her stumble with every other step over the rough terrain. She could just make out where her mother had been weeding the pea patch to get a few things growing again, but otherwise several more weeks would be needed before anything fresh was harvested.

"This is some of the stupidest crap I've ever done," she said, tripping over rocks and tuft grass up the slope. Tiny rivers of water rushed past her, filling holes and trenches that had been dug for house foundations. She flashed the light back and forth across her path as she walked.

The rain was falling the hardest it had all night, the wind picking up, blowing in sideways. Her belly was too big to allow the rain slicker to close in front, forcing her to hold it close to her body as she walked. At one point, the hood was flipped back by the wind, her face and hair instantly drenched with rainwater. She pulled the hood forward again, flashing the light toward the rock pile.

"Come on, where are you guys?" she said into the wind, looking for anything that might be crawling along. "What? Scorpions and centipedes are afraid of a little rain?"

June got to the pile of broken and crushed lava, crouched down for a rock, and looked at it with the flashlight. She decided it was too muddy and tossed it away. Poking around for a cleaner rock, at least one that wasn't covered in mud, she found something craggy, perfect for a bonsai accent. Satisfied with her selection, she looked up at the sky over the mountains. It looked as though the sun was rising on the opposite side of the island.

"Good enough."

She turned for home, flashing the light back and forth before her feet, once again looking for creepy things in the wet dirt.

"What a bunch of little pussies! Bugs don't come out in the rain?"

She stubbed her toe on a rock and pitched forward to her hands and knees.

"Okay, sorry," she said into the wind once she was standing again. "No more name-calling."

She kept stumbling over the loose rocks and gravel on the way down the hill to her house, the silhouette of which was just barely visible in the night sky. She stopped at one of the holes meant to be a foundation for new construction. She waves the light across the surface of the water. "Good place for a swimming pool."

She kept going, still looking for anything scurrying for shelter.

"I gotta tell ya, you guys are a big disappointment. Big fat pregnant girl comes out to your turf and you guys hide."

She got to the back porch and let herself in to the house. Shaking the jacket, she hung it up. June looked down at her feet, wondering how to get the boots off. Just then, the back porch light went on.

"Hey, Dad."

"Get your rock?"

She held up a leg with a boot for him to remove, steadying herself by holding onto the doorknob and window frame in the porch. "Yeah. And not a bug in sight. I guess they all live in the house these days." She wiped rainwater from her face with the back of her hand. "The word is out. Easy livin' at the Kato house."

"We checked the house and it's good. You should've knocked and taken one of us," he said, yanking a wet rubber boot from her foot.

"Yeah, well…"

After he pulled the other free, she went to the sink for a paper towel to dry the rock.

"Get your shower," her mother told her. "Breakfast will be ready soon."

June could smell rice cooking, and a box of old-fashioned oatmeal sat on the counter. Warm rice balls and fruity oatmeal would be perfect for a rainy morning, even if it was in the tropics.

Leaving the light turned off, she took her time in the shower, letting warm water wash away the dirt from the trek in the mud and rain. Finally turning off the water, she pulled the opaque shower curtain back and reached for a towel, ready to step out.

She looked down, and her stomach turned, bringing the taste of bile to her mouth. Instead of spitting up, she screamed. "Jack!"

She realized then he was five miles away.

"Dad!"

She stared down at a scorpion in the middle of the bathroom floor, right where she was about to step. The thing was slowly devouring a large orange centipede, the poisonous kind she had read about the night before. The centipede had been pinched in half, the legs at the back end still trying to propel the body away, while the front end was being consumed by the scorpion.

"Da-ad!"

He appeared at the door and flicked on the light. She pulled the shower curtain across her body, only her face looking out.

She pointed a dripping finger at the floor. "Can you get them out of here?"

He took off a rubber slipper, ready to smack the large scorpion.

"Don't kill it. Just toss him outside."

He got a plastic tub from under the cabinet and scooped the scorpion inside of it, the thing unwilling to let go of its prize. Using toilet paper, he wiped some fluid from where the mini-massacre had occurred.

"It's okay now," he told her, showing her the plastic tub.

"Dad! You mind? I'm in the shower!"

He turned and hurried out, closing the door behind him.

Once she was dressed, she combed her hair straight using the same part the stylist had found, hoping her new style would look good that way after it dried. She used a lightly-scented body spray, for no other reason than to pretend to be pretty. The whole time, she couldn't get the vision from her mind of one poisonous bug eating the other.

In the kitchen, she was put to work at the stove, stirring the pot of oatmeal, enough for two. Her mother dropped chunked papaya into the oatmeal, June stirring it in. It was their latest fad, to try different tropical fruits bought at local markets, trying out different ways of eating them. Mostly, they had become breakfast staples or interesting sauces for dinner noodles.

"Do I want to know what goes on here when I'm not home?" June asked, thinking of how ready her father was to swat the scorpion. Her parents were also vegetarians, the ones that had impressed the habit on her and Amy as kids, something guided by religion. She also knew her father wasn't above eating fish or a burger occasionally.

"Not really."

"Is there much bloodshed?"

"They're bugs. They don't have blood."

"That's not the point," she said, still stirring the oatmeal.

"They don't have souls," her dad said back.

"Are you sure about that?" June mashed down the last of the papaya chunks. "Do you at least take them outside first before killing them?"

"Don't ask questions you might not like the answers to."

One of her favorite comebacks had just been used against her, a line she learned from them, and just like when she was a kid, she had no answer for it.

Her father was already dressed to go out and went for the door. She had forgotten she'd bribed him into spending the day with Rodney.

"You're going now?" she asked.

"I've checked the house again, and the floors are all okay," her dad said from the door.

"That's what you said before. But I found the bull eating the matador on the bathroom floor a little while ago."

Her father didn't answer, only putting on a golf hat that matched the rest of his outfit.

She went to her purse and got some cash for him to take. "Just make sure Rodney has fun."

June watched as her mother kissed him goodbye.

"He has a little extra spring in his step today," June muttered, going back to her breakfast.

Just like her father, her mother didn't answer, only putting more oatmeal in June's bowl.

"I thought we were going out for breakfast? Or is this one of Dad's tricks to get me to eat breakfast twice today?"

"It took him a few months to figure it out. I want to go to Ka'ahu's in town on the way to your friend's house."

June wasn't sure if it was the combination of the fruit and oatmeal, or if she was actually hungry for a change, but she ate everything that had been made for her, along with two slices of bread with peanut butter. By the time she was done with the dishes, she was fantasizing about Ka'ahu's menu.

***

Once her mother had a basket of snacks and drinks packed, they left. After adjustments to mirrors and the bench seat in the pickup, they bounced down the gravelly driveway to the main road.

"We need to go through town and out past the airport," June told her, looking at the map on her lap. She'd used a yellow highlighter to draw a line from their house to Paia on the opposite side of the island.

They followed along the two-lane highway, June watching out the window of the pickup as surfers plied waves and shore fishermen watched their lines. Pickups were parked here and there along the road, guys and gals sitting inside, watching sets of waves tumble in, June wondering what exactly they watched for. She knew how to surf, mostly how to stay up on a board, but that was about it. It was something she planned on doing more of later for the exercise. The rainstorm from the night before was barely over and the parks were already filling with locals preparing for picnics and tourists looking for suntans.

They got through the short tunnel and made the bend around toward town, chatting quietly about the scheduled date of her delivery in about a week and a half.

"Divya wants me there Monday morning, check in, do some blood work, and go to maternity. I really want a nice, easygoing delivery. I don't want drama. Just like Mick said, this isn't something I need to screw up."

"What's Mick got to do with it?" her mom asked.

"Nothing. He just said I need to pay attention to what's right in front of me, what's most important."

"Your baby and delivery isn't any of his business."

"I know. It's just that...he gave me a pep talk on the phone last night."

"Fine. But you're doing this with us. Your life is here, not somewhere else."

June bit her tongue until it was time to point out the turn in town that took them toward the airport. There had been one or two insinuations from her parents in the last few months that Mick could possibly be the father and not Jack. Not wanting to revisit that, June took a series of slow deep breaths, the last turning to a sigh, a habit she was still trying to break.

"Anyway, since the pregnancy has been going so well, Divya has downgraded me from high-risk to high-normal. But she's still going to induce Monday morning, and once I get my epidural, it hopefully won't take too long after that."

"May Twenty-second. That's a Gemini," her mother said.

"Yes. So?"

"A good communicator. A couple of days earlier and it would be a Taurus, the bull."

"I'm not sure which is worse for me," June said. "Someone that will talk and argue with me constantly over every little detail, or someone bull-headed about everything?"

They rode along quietly for a few minutes.

"What about Jack?" her mother asked.

"I'm supposed to call him once labor has started."

"What do you want me and Dad to do?"

More power and control being returned.

"You can keep my phone and field Amy's calls and to give Jack updates once things start to roll. I'll show you how to take pictures to send to them. Dad can pace or do whatever he does. I don't remember what he did when Amy delivered."

"Got in the way, mostly. Same as when I had you kids. I'll try to keep him busy."

"Maybe he can be the one to talk to Jack while you keep Amy pacified. They like each other."

"I'm surprised Amy hasn't shown up here to direct things," Mabel said.

"I wish she could be," June said after a moment. "I can't believe I'm having my baby without her here."

Mabel gripped June's hand reassuringly.

"I don't know how I got through these last eight months without her."

And there it was, the impetus for the morning's second round of tears. The first came when she stubbed her toe while rock collecting in the dark, when she was so close to breaking one of Divya's late-term maternity rules. She was supposed to be resting; even going to work was bending the rules. Rock hunting in a storm was definitely off the table to an obstetrician. This second time the reason for her tears was even harder to bear: not having her lifelong best friend and twin sister with her for the birth of her baby.

June blotted a teardrop from the map. "Sorry for all the crying lately, Mom."

"Should've seen me in those last few weeks carrying you and Amy. Even she had her moments. You don't remember?"

"Amy cried about something? She must've hid that from me."

"It's no secret how you guys are with each other. No one could ever come between you two, not us or a husband. All this will settle pretty soon."

"I'm ready for that, any time." Now that her emotions were under control, June looked at her watch. "We still have time to eat again."

"You're hungry already?"

"I think the kid is getting the first helping of everything these days."

Mabel turned the car for the mall, parking near the restaurant that was quickly becoming a family favorite on the island. They were quickly seated in a booth when the hostess saw the size of June's belly. Without looking at a menu, June ordered two orders of burnt toast, while her mother got coffee.

"We don't have to see this woman, Dear. I'd rather see you rest today."

"No, she's expecting us. And I went out in the rain to get that dumb rock."

"What exactly is the rock for?"

"Who knows? She asked for it, so I'm bringing it. She only said she had some ideas for how to deal with scorpions. Considering she lives out in the middle of a sugar cane field, and the size of her extended family, who am I to ignore the advice of an expert?"

When her mother asked, June gave the long story about meeting Auntie Haunani and the Baxter family the year before, and the basics of what she'd learned about kahuna, something the elderly woman was known for.

"But don't call her a witch doctor," June said, finishing her toast.

"You're not getting mixed up in anything mystical, are you?"

"No, Mom. I'm still a good little Buddhist. Always have been, always will be."

"One thing I've never heard you talk about, is if Maui is turning out to be as good as what you thought?" her mother asked.

"Certainly different from what I planned. LA was stressing me out, no secret about that. Something had to give and I didn't want it to be my mind. So, after that quickie vacation, I decided I liked Maui well enough to move here. I gave up a lot back home to start over. I'm not nearly as busy at work, but for now, that's okay. I certainly never planned on being a single mother, though."

"It'll work out, Dear."

"I know. I just have to take one day at a time. It's just that some of these days aren't so easy right now, and becoming rather unpredictable."

"You do like your predictability."

"Ha! You sound like Amy. She keeps reminding me how I had my whole life planned out years in advance. Then Jack came along and turned everything upside-down. Now, the baby."

"Your father and I are quite proud of how well you're coping with it all."

June put some money in the black folder to pay the check. "I'm coping?"

"Aren't you?"

"If spending all my spare time in the bathroom is coping, then yes, I'm doing quite well. Speaking of bathrooms, it's that time again."

***

June watched as they went past old cane fields. She saw a sign, part of the directions. "There's Baldwin Avenue. We're supposed to turn there and go up the hill past the town."

Paia, the little town they were driving through, was wrapped in layers of quaintness, injected with a heavy dose of tourist trap, and floated in signs for water activities. Only a few thousand people, the small storefronts and old plantation-style homes were leftover from older agricultural times, when Maui was more famous for sugar production, and before surfing had become a rage. The sport of windsurfing was invented in the ocean only steps away, and other than restaurants catering to tourists, water sports were now the main moneymaker for the town.

The town stretched up the hill for a short way until only bright green fields faced them on either side of the road, sugar cane leaves glistening with rainwater yet to evaporate.

"Slow down. If we get to Rainbow Park, we've gone too far," June said, reading her notes. "There's some little road we turn down that goes into the fields."

"Is there a sign?" asked Mabel looking intently out the windshield.

"She didn't say."

"How do we know where to turn?"

June looked at her watch. It was almost noon, the time they were supposed to be there.

"I don't know, Mom," June said, holding the impatience from her voice. "Just watch for something that looks like a driveway, I guess."

Few other cars were out. They found the sign that indicated they were in Rainbow Park. Mable turned the pickup around and coasted down the hill, both of them looking for anything that might look like a driveway to someone's home.

June looked at the map, but the rock in her other hand caught her eye.

"Wait," June said. Mabel applied the brakes and eased to a stop in the middle of the road. June pointed with the rock in her hand. "That rock cairn over there. That's got to be the place to turn."

Mabel turned onto the narrow dirt road, more watery mud holes than firm dirt.

"Put it in first, Mom."

She down shifted and they crept along, bouncing through mud holes and over rocks.

"Careful of the holes. I don't want to break my water out here." June clung to the door grip to steady herself. "Better to go slow and around the puddles than through them."

"I know how to drive a truck, Dear," Mabel said impatiently. "I delivered a lot of flowers over the last several decades."

June rolled her eyes and clamped her teeth. "On paved roads in LA, not dirt roads on Maui."

After a few minutes, they saw the rusted, corrugated steel roof of an old house poking above leafy greenery of sugar cane growing wild. A large tree loomed over the house, and when they got closer, June saw it was an ancient jacaranda, just beginning to bloom.

"Is this the right place?"

"I don't see any other houses out here."

"Go in?" Mabel asked when they got to an open spot in a low lava rock wall that surrounded the house.

"I'm pretty sure she doesn't offer curbside service."

Her mother drove in. No other vehicles were around, and June wondered if anyone was home. With no name or signs anywhere at the front of the house, she still wasn't sure if they'd found the right place.

"No reason to be like that, June."

"Like what?"

"Always so snippy."

"Why does everybody keep saying that?" June wiped sweat from her face. "Dad says I'm crabby. Amy says I'm in a mood. You say I'm snippy. Mick said I'm in a funk. You know what I have to say?"

"I have a good idea, and there's no reason to. The baby can hear everything you say."

June pointed to a place to park in the shade. "Like any kid of mine is going to grow up wholesome."

As soon as they stopped, a dog sat up on the shady front porch and barked a few times. They stayed in the car.

"Ili! Kuli kuli!" someone yelled from inside the house. June noticed the front door was open but the screen door closed at the front. A tiny figure in a green flowery mu'u mu'u came to the door, rubbed the dog's head and gave it a bone. "You dat hapai malihini?"

June and her mom looked at each other.

"Hapai?" her mother asked.

"It means pregnant," June said back with a shrug. "I thought malihini was a fish."

Satisfied the dog was busy with a bone and might not chase her, June pushed her way out of the pickup. Out of habit, she looked at the ground for scorpions before stepping out.

"Yes, I'm June Kato." She swung the pickup door closed so the lady could see her belly. "I called you yesterday. You said be here at noon."

"Come." The old lady stepped back into the house again but waited behind the screen door.

June and her mother began to walk to the porch.

"You bring pohaku?" the old woman asked.

June reached into her large woven bag for the rock. All she had brought in the bag were two bottles of water, and packages of crackers, phone, and the clutch she had been using the last few days. She held the rock up for the woman to see.

"Toss'em on that pile," she instructed June, pointing with a finger to a rock pile in the corner of the yard. It was something of a trail cairn, and June set her rock carefully at the top.

June went to the porch, her mother right behind. Several chickens pranced about, looking for anything to eat in the dirt. A few hibiscus plants bloomed in cheerful yellows and reds at either side of the front porch. They took the steps up to the covered porch, keeping a wary eye on the dog. It was a mutt of some sort, half a dozen different breeds and colorings in its shaggy coat. It looked up at June for a moment panting, flopped its tail twice, and went back to gnawing its bone.

"Ili okay," the woman said. "Friendly kind dog."

June tried to bend over to rub the dog's ears but couldn't get low enough. Both of them waited on the porch for an invitation from the old woman to come in.

"You want visit me, you need come in," the woman said from behind the screen door.

June opened the door, they kicked their shoes off, and went in the dark house. Not a single light was on anywhere, and she could barely see. It took a moment for June's eyes to adjust to the dark interior before following the woman to another covered porch at the back of the house.

Haunani was even skinnier than what June remembered, someone that shouldn't go outside on a blustery day. Her hair had more salt than pepper in it, braided into a long rope and turned around several times at the top of her head, with a tiny flower tucked in at one side. Her skin was dark brown, and ancient smile lines and crow's feet had become signs of distinction and wisdom. One set of kukui beads hung loosely from around her neck, along with a green lei braided from leaves. She couldn't be more than a few years different in age from her mother. The more June looked at her, the more familiar she seemed.

When they had first met months before, June had learned a few things about Hawaiian kahuna. She'd also learned that Auntie Haunani was the top kahuna on the island. She was known as a Kahuna la'au lapa'au, a healer adept in herbal medicine, and also as a kahuna hoohapai, someone that focused on pregnancy issues. These were time-honored traditions, and people like Haunani carried them on into the present day.

"Not many days for you," Auntie Haunani said after settling in cushioned lawn chairs. "So soon for you."

June sat, and rubbed her belly. "Two weeks tomorrow."

"No so long, I think."

"Well, that's when…"

June's mother gave her an elbow to be quiet.

"And not so big. Good thing no more twins."

"No, no twins this time," June said back, wondering where the conversation was going. She wasn't there for pregnancy, but to ask questions about the scorpions. She fidgeted in her chair, trying to find a comfortable position.

"You want go shishi?"

"I really got to go pee," June said.

The woman pointed an arthritic finger down a hall.

June tried to listen from inside the bathroom, if she had been sent away so Auntie Haunani could have a private chat with her mother. She heard muttering voices, but couldn't pick out topics or even individual words. She gave them a chance to gossip, if that's what they were doing, before returning.

Her mother was standing, her purse in her hand. The nut lei the kahuna was wearing was now around her mother's neck. "I'll wait on the porch while you talk," she told June and excused herself with a smile to the old woman.

"Why you come see me?" the woman asked quietly.

June expected something entirely different from what she was finding in the home of a kahuna. Maybe incense burning, symbolic imagery, chanting music playing softly, a gruff old woman acting as though she had something else better to do than meet a neurotic pregnant woman. What she got instead was a pleasant-tempered woman with an easy smile, perched in a lawn chair on her back porch.

"I'm not sure."

"You come all dis way just to talk story with old lady?"

"I'm sorry, I…"

"Don't be sorry."

"Okay."

"And don't be so agreeable."

June didn't know what to think or say. She couldn't be sorry, and she couldn't be agreeable.

"I came because I am afraid of the scorpions in my house," she told Auntie Haunani directly.

"Afraid for keiki get sting?"

"Yeah."

"Best thing, use hard kind shoe to smack'em."

"I don't want to kill them, just keep them out of the house and keep the baby safe after it comes."

Her answer went ignored. "Not know sex of the keiki?"

"No, I…"

"You want for Auntie tell?"

Auntie Haunani moved her chair to next to June, lifting her shirt and slipping her hand beneath. June was surprised when the woman ran her thick, coarse hand over her taut skin, gently touching her belly button.

Auntie smiled. "You want know?"

"I can wait."

"What names you got?"

"Logan Aito, if it's a boy. Melanie Aiko, if it's a girl."

A giant smile burst onto Auntie's face. "Gentle names for brave child."

As the kahuna felt June's belly with her hand, the baby began to kick.

"I'm not so sure about how gentle a child of mine is going to be with a kick like that," June said.

They talked about the baby, its habit of kicking, and using June's bladder as a chaise lounge. She ran her hand over June's proud belly one last time before pulling her blouse down again.

"Still got rock and ti plants at home?" Auntie Haunani asked.

June smiled. "You remember that?" While June was taking care of Kekoa, Haunani's nephew, a large rock appeared in June's front yard just near the front door. With each passing day while she treated him, flowery leis had been draped over the rock, until Kekoa recovered. "Yes, still there, and we try to put a flower on it, when we remember. Was that you who put it there?"

Haunani smiled. "Things happen sometimes without explanation."

"They sure have been these last few weeks."

"You still eating poi?"

"When we find it at farmers markets. It's one of the few things I can eat that stays down. Might not become a regular part of my diet after the baby comes, though."

"No need then."

They sat quietly for a while, drinking lemonade.

"You crying all the time?" Haunani asked gently.

"Yeah." June blushed, and lowered her head. "Not really like me to cry so much."

"Go ahead and cry. Dis best time of your life! Okay to cry all over everything!" Auntie took June's hand in hers. Somehow, June knew the time had come for some teaching, the reason for her visit. "That place you live, long time sugar cane field. Those bugs, they got right live there, too. Just like people, they like live indoors. Easy way, yeah? But good you patient with them, not kill them. They learn be patient with you, too."

"Is there a way I can keep them out of the house?" June asked, afraid to interrupt.

"Tutu say you believe in things?"

They had indeed gossiped about her while June was in the bathroom. "What kind of things?"

"Aumakua…family spirits."

"I suppose."

"You still talk story with your Granny, Grampy?"

June looked down at her fingers, nervously wrestling with each other. She willed them to stop. "Yeah."

"How long they been gone?" Haunani asked quietly.

"Twenty years."

"Good girl. Good lesson to teach keiki, to keep the ancestors close. You know, ancestors never too far away. Best to let them hang around."

Auntie Haunani pushed up from her chair and collected a small rock from a basket, handing it to June.

"Keep that under crib, all the time. Bugs no like that kind rock."

June gave it a quick examination before stowing it in her bag.

"No one else to touch that rock but you. Very important."

June wondered how she was going to keep her father's curiosity at bay. "Okay."

"Other ancient Hawaiian thing you can do to keep bugs out of crib, go to store, get four big kind funnels." She held her hands up to show the size. "Shove'm up da legs of crib, upside-down way. Bugs no get past those."

June chuckled. "That's the ancient Hawaiian way? To use plastic funnels?"

"Works good!"

There was warmth about the woman's eyes, and maybe the slightest twinkle as though she knew something she wasn't letting on about. But June didn't want to know any more about the baby than what she already did, only that there was only one inside her, breaking something of a family trait. She couldn't help keep from bursting with one last question. June knew then that if anybody could answer her question, Auntie Haunani could.

"Is my baby healthy?"

Another giant smile, which was all the answer June needed.

***

Mabel helped Auntie Haunani prepare lunch in the kitchen while June sat at the table and listened to them chat. Somehow, the woman knew to make only vegetarian foods, or maybe that's what she ate ordinarily. There were field greens that looked as though they came from a pea patch, small flakey rolls that were reportedly left over from another day but tasted fresh, and a tiny pan-fried burrito filled with banana.

"These are so good," June said, eating the third skinny burrito. She knew it was a favorite Filipino food, often filled with meat, so she avoided them whenever there had been a hospital potluck.

"Banana lumpia. Good for hapai girls."

"I've heard the other way around, that banana lumpia is good for getting girls pregnant?" June asked.

"Maybe good for both ways," the old woman said.

June ate one last lumpia before washing it down with water. "Mom, you gotta learn how to make these."

Haunani gave a simple recipe for making the things.

"Auntie, what do you know about shooting stars and comets in Hawaiian folklore?" June asked, feeling stuffed.

"Stars, in the sky, dat way," the woman said, waving her hand in a general direction. They had been on so many roads that day, June had lost her sense of direction. "Big event coming up."

"Yes, a comet will be visible. Does it have anything to do with scorpions? Or with all the scorpion stings lately?"

"Scorpions?" Haunani gave it some thought. "Only that comets were sometimes feared by the ancients. Shooting stars are special time. Interesting your baby coming at same time as comet."

"Why is that interesting?"

"Historic occasion brings special child."

Now June was worried. "What do you mean, special?"

“Wait to see until grown up.” Haunani shrugged. “Nothing else.”

June was getting frustrated with the cryptic messages from the elderly woman. All she really wanted to know was why the scorpions were making such a mess of things on Maui right then. She took the piece of parchment paper she’d been given by Marilyn Scanlon from her purse and unfolded it.

Auntie Haunani frowned down at the paper June had spread on the table. “Where you get that from?”

June was startled at the woman’s sudden turn in mood. “Someone gave it to me.”

Auntie snatched the paper away and crumpled it into a ball, setting it out of June’s reach.

“That haole woman in town, yeah? You no more visit her. Those kind people bad news.”

“Okay.”

June was startled that the woman knew who the paper came from, until she saw Auntie Haunani’s face soften again. The old woman had nothing more to say about the comet and the rise of scorpions, or June’s baby.

They got to the end of the meal, and June watched as the last of the uneaten lumpia were wrapped in foil. Those and several of the biscuits were put in a bag.

“Auntie,” June said when the bag of food was given to her. She dug through her bag for her wallet. “I’ve taken a lot of your time. You helped me a lot. Is there…”

“Uku no need,” the woman said to interrupt June from offering money. “You bring keiki here for Auntie to hold. That my uku.”

“Okay,” June said with a smile. “What’s a good day to call?”

"Auntie always home. No need call, just bring keiki any kind time."

June blushed, and felt like crying right then, but she didn't know why.

***

It was mid-afternoon by the time they got back to town. Something had been bugging June ever since reading in the newspaper about the most recent venomous death, and meeting Marilyn Scanlon. There were entirely too many coincidences in this scorpion business, and instead of relying on news articles, women in caftans, or a kindly old lady living in the middle of a sugar cane field, she decided to gather whatever clinical evidence might be available. Maybe that was the real reason she had her mother drive her to town. If Detective Atkins from MPD wanted evidence of foul play, she was going to find it for him.

June saw the so-called 'mall hospital' off to the side, barely a block from the mall itself.

"Mom, I'll buy us something to drink if you let me do a quick errand?"

Getting an agreement, June had her mother park the car near the front entrance to the hospital. She went in, leaving her mother to wait in the car. After a quick stop at the information desk, she took the elevator down to the basement level. Stepping out, there was a sign on the wall indicating the morgue was off to the left.

June was the only one inside the small waiting area of the morgue. She hoped her pregnant belly was hidden behind the high counter. Above the counter was a thick glass partition, something that looked bulletproof. She got a sense of security, having the extra layer of something to hide behind. There was a large measure of death on the other side of that partition. Being a doctor for so many years, she was no stranger to death, but carrying a child, the promise of new life, she got a shiver thinking about the work that went on only a few steps away. She gave the small bell on the counter several whacks, waiting for someone to come out.

When a young woman came out, June flashed her hospital ID, keeping her thumb over the name of the hospital she worked at, instead allowing the blue caduceus to show. "Yeah, hi. I'm Doctor Kato, here to check some records on recent deceased." She quickly put the ID away again.

"Who are they?" the girl asked, preparing to write names on a paper.

"The women with the scorpion stings. Are they still here?"

"Still waiting until families can be notified. Then they'll be sent to morticians or shipped home. Why?"

"I need to review their hospital records, please," she said, trying to sound impatient and officious. If there was one thing she knew how to do in a medical setting, it was to look mildly perturbed over nothing at all.

When the clerk had June sign in, she thought to scribble her name just enough to make it somewhat illegible. It took a few more minutes for the clerk to find the charts. The clerk wandered off again when June told her she could read them there at the counter.

She made a few notes, dates of death, care provider names at the hospital, next of kin last names. She compared procedures and lab tests run for each. One common thing she did see was that pharmaceutical toxicology screens had not been run on the four women that had died at the mall hospital, only venom tox screens. Each was positive for having an unspecified arachnid venom. In each, the admitting diagnosis was the same as post mortem cause of death--anaphylactic reaction to venomous sting. Half an hour of reading led her nowhere.

She gave the bell another whack. Her next move had to be clever.

"You still have blood samples, right?" June asked the morgue clerk when she came back.

The sullen clerk nodded, and June got the idea she didn't like her job much.

"I want full pharmacologic tox screens run for each patient. Bill the county, and send the results to this email."

It was no secret each woman had been stung by a scorpion; there had to have been something else in their system at the same time that made the venom so much more potent. Or maybe the venom was much more powerful than normal, indicating a new subspecies was emerging. She had considered that before, but why would they attack pregnant women and seemingly no one else? There had to be something else in the pregnant women's blood stream that made them so susceptible to the venom.

June gave the generic email address for her clinic at her hospital, hoping that somehow her name would remain hidden.

"Basic results would be ready tomorrow, but a full screen would be done on Oahu, and might take as long as two weeks."

"I can wait. But make sure I get those early results tomorrow."

"You need to see the bodies?" the clerk asked.

June gave it a thought, wondering if she was up to viewing dead bodies. It was something she hadn't prepared herself for that day, not expecting the invitation. When June nodded, the clerk hit a buzzer, unlocking an electronic door for June to pass through.

"From the charts, it looked like all the stings were on the arms?" June asked, following behind the clerk.

"Don't know. I never look too close at the bodies. I just handle paperwork."

The clerk checked a record number, comparing it to a metal drawer. She pulled the cooler drawer open, June getting an instant chill. The chill wasn't from the cold room, but from the sight of the body bag in the long drawer. The victim inside was either extremely portly or pregnant. June knew which.

A tag was checked on the outside of a rubberized bag, which was then zipped open by the clerk wearing rubber gloves. She groped around inside to pull back a plastic sheet, exposing only the mottled gray forearm. Even though she'd worked in health care for twenty years, June had never seen the corpse of a pregnant woman. The banana lumpia she'd eaten at Auntie Haunani's home were beginning to turn in her stomach.

The girl used both hands to wrench around the stiff arm for June to see the injured wrist. June looked as closely as she would let her belly get. Sure enough, there was a raised welt, also gray, with a pencil point puncture in the middle, right over the thumb side of the wrist. If the woman had been alive, the welt would've been red.

There was another wrapped body in the same drawer, and the clerk went through the same routine of unwrapping. June took a look at each victim's lifeless gray arm, the sting punctures looking alike. The most compelling thing about them, though, was the placement of the sting, right over the large artery of the wrist.

June considered that possibly the venom had been injected directly into the bloodstream, each woman's heart and brain being flooded with a toxic dose of venom. It could've caused something called 'speed shock', a dose of something that would otherwise be survivable if the sting had been into skin. Absorption of the toxin through skin circulation would've been delayed, much slower than directly into an artery or vein, the same as an injection of medication. But with the injuries of these two women right into the bloodstream, once a bolus of the toxin hit the heart or brain, there would be an instant shutdown, a collapse of all organ systems. Maybe that's what had happened with a large enough dose, and the venom had been more powerful than usual for scorpions. It wasn't much different from a heroin addict unknowingly injecting a very pure form of the drug and instantly dying from the overdose. Even though they might be a chronic user, their body couldn't handle the massive amount of drug all at once.

"Show me their faces," June muttered.

She gulped as the young woman unzipped the bag up to the top and folded back the inner plastic wrapping. The woman was young, her flesh gray, her blond hair combed back from her face. Her eyes lifelessly peered out at the world through narrow slits. Had she been alive, she would've been pretty.

The second was middle-aged, Asian, one eye open more than the other, equally as pretty, yet still only a mannequin of a former person. It was as if she were looking at herself.

June wanted to vomit.

She turned away. "Tell the diener I also need cutdowns and microphotos of each sting wound, and to send those to the same email address."

June rushed out of the morgue. Even though the cool room felt good, the stink of formaldehyde was too much to breathe safely, and the image of dead gray faces was hard to bear. Possibly the worst image of all was the obvious pregnant belly that couldn't be hidden by plastic wraps within the body bag. Walking through the sunshine to her mother waiting in the pickup warmed her, the tropical breeze clearing a few of the images away.

"Something to drink?" June asked after they reparked and entered the mall.

"Do we have time for shopping?" her mother asked. "I called Dad and told him we might be late for dinner."

"Oh, so that's how it works?" June asked, thinking of the spat from the day before. "Just call and say I'll be late?"

"Better than telling us nothing at all."

Their first stop was in the baby clothes store, a place June had hit hard a few times before. At first, she had a hard time shaking the images of dead women from her mind, but after browsing through sale tables and feeling a few strong kicks inside her, she was able to refocus on this new task of shopping for baby clothes. It took almost no time to find some onesies in various sizes for the baby. It was when she paid that she noticed the colors of them were either yellow or pink, nothing blue.

She waited on a mall bench while her mother shopped for shoes. It gave her time to consider what she'd learned at the morgue.

"I know pregnant women emit pheromones that supposedly make men horny. That's in all the brochures and literature that Divya gave me to read about what to expect during pregnancy. But could those same pheromones attract scorpions somehow? Or other pheromones that haven't been detected or identified?" She watched as a pregnant teenager walked past arm in arm with her boyfriend, also a teenager. "If so, why haven't there been reports of women in deserts or other tropical places dying from stings?"

Once again, it made no sense. The more she thought of reasons why pregnant women would be getting stung at such a high rate in a small place like Maui, the less she thought the problem was occurring naturally.

Their other stop was at the coffee and smoothie shop. June had a large banana, guava, and spirolina smoothie, while her mother had iced coffee. June eyed the coffee wantonly.

"In a couple of weeks, Dear, you'll be able to have coffee again.

She had felt almost continuous kicking ever since getting to the mall, that maybe a shopping trip was too much. It was definitely too much for her back. "If I gave this kid coffee right now, I don't know what would happen." She looked down at her large paper cup, feeling the cold, sweaty sides with her fingertips. She chased one last morgue image from her thoughts. "But this smoothie is so good."

June wiped some sweat from her brow, even though the indoor mall was naturally air-conditioned by breezes from outside. Even her hair was sweaty, which she tried tucking behind her ears.

"It's pretty, what you had done," her mother said.

"Thanks. I doubt Dad even noticed. I like how a few of the highlights still remain at the ends in front. Sort of playful," June said, finishing her smoothie. "Not that there's anything playful about me anymore."

"Pretty for your face. Amy said she's thinking of a major overhaul."

"And she'll look fantastic, as always." She looked at her mother's hair. "You haven't had your hair done since you got here."

"No time." She shrugged, exactly the same way June does. "Anyway, don't know where to go here. The only place near us is at the resort across the highway from us. There's no need to pay resort salon prices for white hair."

"It's not completely white." June wiped her face with a napkin again, still trying to get the gray image of death out of her mind. Her back hurt and she was hot. She needed better air conditioning, or some way to cool off. "Come on, Mom. I have an idea."

They were quickly back in the car, June pointing directions to another part of town.

"Where are we going?"

"To the salon I went to yesterday. Pretty soon, you'll be holding a brand new grandbaby in your arms, and you'll want to look your best for the pictures." She pointed to the exit out of the parking lot. "And the idea of having cool water flowing over my head right now is about as close to bliss as I'm gonna get for a while."

June was worried the place might be closed on a Sunday afternoon. Koreans were like that, restaurants, salons, shops would close on Sundays, but worked late hours the rest of the week to make up for it. June found she was holding her breath as they got closer to the place. She'd been there only once but already it was a place of respite for her, a place where she could relax and not take the rest of the world too seriously, if only for an hour or so. When she saw the open sign in the front window, she breathed a sigh of relief. There was even a parking spot right in the front.

"How'd you find this place?" her mother asked, giving the small shop a closer look once they parked.

"Just walking by, had to pee, and went in."

"It's okay?"

"It looks a little rough on the outside but the gals running the place are nice. Come on."

The narrow commercial street was even quieter on Sunday afternoon than it had been during the week, and few cars were parked at the curb. When they got out, June could see the same stylist inside, bringing a smile to her face for the first time since leaving Auntie Haunani's house.

"You're back!" Myong said.

"You have time for a new customer?"

"Always!" Myong went to Mabel and greeted her in Korean for some reason. Mabel had something to say back, also in Korean.

June was stunned, hearing her mother speak Korean. "Mom, you know Korean?"

"Some. Long story. I'll tell you later."

Myong lead Mabel away to the shampoo sink. "If you want, you can sit in the other stylist's chair. It's more comfortable than those chairs in the waiting area," she said to June.

As much as her mother getting some overdue attention, June had hoped to get another relaxing scalp massage and cool water shampoo. With only one stylist working, she'd have to wait until her mother was done. While she did, she read a gossip magazine while listening to her mother gossip with the teenager in Korean. Here was a surprise that she had a hard time reconciling, that her mother spoke Korean so well. It wasn't long before she tuned them out, allowing her eyes get heavy. In the mid-afternoon, it would take almost no effort to drift off to sleep.

At least until Kim showed up at her side. As quick as that, they went to the shampoo sink, while her mother and Myong cheerfully chatted at the styling station.

"You like what Myong did yesterday?" Kim asked June while rinsing her hair at the sink.

June had to force her eyes open from the deep relaxation she was feeling. "I do."

"It certainly suits your face. You could use a little more fullness. Maybe after the baby comes, you'll come in for a body perm?"

"I've tried it before. It's just that my hair has so little natural body, it doesn't hold up."

By the time Kim was done with June's shampoo, Myong was already halfway through with her mother's cut. They continued chatting in Korean, her mother still doing a decent job of keeping up. Today, the process was going much more quickly than with June's cut the day before, maybe because Kim wasn't supervising every little move Myong made.

"Your mom speaks Korean pretty good," Kim said to June while waving the blow dryer through her hair. She must have been eavesdropping, although June didn't know a word of the language.

"Yeah, you never know what kind of surprise is waiting when you get up in the morning."

Once the hair was mostly dry, Kim combed June's hair, trying to find the same part. "Anything else?"

Just then, June saw a familiar sight out the front window from the corner of her eye, a woman dressed in a caftan. The woman stopped, looked in the window, and waved.

"Crap," June muttered upon seeing Marilyn Scanlon, wondering if she was going to get interrogated about her fake visit to Katrina, the other birth angel she was supposed to go to.

Marilyn came in and breezed over to where June sat in the chair. Kim backed off, taking several steps back.

"Aiko? Is that you, Aiko?" Marilyn said with a highly sweetened voice and a plastic smile.

"Pardon me?" June said in her ordinary, unaccented voice. She kept the foreign tone out this time, giving up on the pretense she was native Japanese.

Marilyn shifted her eyes from June's face to the prominent belly. "You're Aiko, right?"

She looked up at the towering Marilyn standing uncomfortably close. "I'm sorry. My name is June," she said squarely.

"But I could've sworn…you didn't come visit me the other day?"

"Her name is June," Mabel said from the next chair over. "I should know. I'm her mother, and I gave her that name."

Marilyn looked confused, but headed for the door.

"You go now!" Kim said sharply. "Go on! You go now!"

After Marilyn was gone, Myong went to the door and put up the closed sign and lowered the blinds a bit. June could see Kim was visibly shaken by something, and when she began combing June's hair, it was too brusquely. The last thing June wanted was an angry woman working near her head.

Kim stopped combing and went to the counter below the mirror. June was relieved when she found a curling iron to plug in instead of something sharp.

"I no like that woman!" Kim said sharply, aiming her hand at the door Marilyn left through a moment before. She held up two fingers for June to see. "Two of my friends go see her. Nothing done for them, but charge them anyway! Complete fraud! I no like her!"

Kim touched the iron to test the temperature and collected the comb again. This time the combing was more controlled.

"What they call it for crummy doctors? Quacks? They still use that word? Quack?"

"Um, yeah, I think so. Fraud, quack, scam artist. Lots of words for it," June said back, hoping the sudden seizure of Kim's emotions was over.

"Okay, done with that problem. What kind of curls do you want?" Kim asked.

June pulled a lock of her hair out and looked at it cross-eyed. "Give it some lift. Maybe what you would do if you gave me a body perm."

"That's what Myong said yesterday, that it would look good on you."

They talked about what Kim could do for something 'girlish', to use her words, before getting started with the hot iron. Almost right away, June was regretting the use of something hot so close to her.

"Your two friends, Kim, what happened to them?" June asked. "The ones that went to that woman?"

"They go see her. Just blah blah blah, all talk but no work. Like some sort of fortune teller! Then she wanted to be their whatchamacallit…"

"Birth angel?"

Kim pointed. "That's right. But my friends, they were wise to it. Just a big scam, you know? They paid their money just to get out and never went back."

"I see." It sounded like the exact same scenario June went through with Marilyn, the fake pregnancy assessment with the pebbles and parchment paper, followed by the so-called aura massage. "And it was with that woman?"

"Exactly her. Good thing for my friends, they used fake names when they went to see her."

"Yes, that was a good idea." June closed her eyes, trying to pretend the heat from the iron was actually Jack's fingers in her hair. It had been since the day before that she'd thought of him, and a week since she'd fantasized about his touch on her body. The warmth and movement in her hair, the occasional touch to her cheek, was something June tried turning into a daydream. When she felt her head get nudged forward for Kim to start in the back, and the soft touch on her neck, it felt the same as Jack's lips in a dark bedroom. She wasn't sure if she was smiling, and if she was, if it mattered. She was lost in something pleasant for a change, and even the baby seemed quiet right then. In the quiet salon, it wasn't long until she felt like she could nap.

In only a few minutes, Kim was done. Somehow, the few simple waves and her hair being teased at the back had taken years of age off June's face, a bit of an instant boost to her morale.

Myong finished at the same time. June looked at her mother; the old perm had been removed, replaced by a layered style more commonly worn by women much younger. With a little makeup, her mother would look twenty years younger than her real age.

"Mom! You should leave Dad and find a younger guy!"

"Don't give me any ideas."

Mabel overpaid, the same that June had done the day before. By the time they were in the car and driving out of town, it was almost dark.

"You think Dad got Rodney something to eat?" she asked.

"Even if they did eat, he'll want dinner as soon as we're home. Your dad won't go hungry for long."

"Hopefully he's getting something started. I'm hungry again."

"Who was the lady that came in the shop?" Mabel finally asked, June expecting it much sooner.

June slouched down in her seat, some of the air going out of the afternoon. "I saw her yesterday. She was the massage therapist I went to see."

"So, that's why you were gone so long. But why Aiko? Isn't that the name you used a long time ago in Japan?"

June rolled up the window and turned on the A/C so she wouldn't have to talk over the noise of the wind blowing in. Feeling a gentle kick, she caressed her belly, waiting impatiently for the baby to come. All she wanted to do was hold the baby close to her breast for its first meal and sleep together. But she had more almost two weeks to wait and an explanation to give to her mother.

"Just the name I used working for that Japanese cosmetics company. It comes in handy sometimes if I need to keep my real identity to myself."

"But why are you keeping your real name a secret? And how did you meet that woman? The hairstylist sure didn't like her."

"I found her name and information from some brochures, as some sort of New Age birthing assistant. I never was going to use that woman's services. I was just curious about what those so-called birth angels do. There's something that just doesn't measure up with them."

"And you're on one of your crusades again?"

"No! Not at all. I just want to be safe. That's why we went all the way out to Auntie Haunani's place today."

"That's changing the subject. Why'd you go to that woman's office if you think there's something suspicious about her? That doesn't sound safe to me."

June adjusted the seatbelt placement over her body, trying to delay answering. "Okay. So, from what I've heard, a couple of the women that died from scorpion stings went to those birth angel women. That's way too much of a coincidence to be ignored."

"It is one of your crusades then?"

June picked at a fingernail. "Yeah, I suppose."

"Leave it alone, Dear," her mother told her. "You have an OB you like, and just concentrate on these last few days."

"Yeah." June settled her picking and clasped her hands together, willing them to stop the nervous activity. "What'd you think of Auntie Haunani?"

"She seemed very warm-hearted," Mabel said. "What did she tell you?"

"Kind of private. Just like why you know Korean. None of each other's' business."

"Just leave all that birth angel stuff alone for now."

"Yeah, Mom, I will."

"Seriously. Don't get involved in it. Just like you said, it seems like there's something going on behind the scenes, and you don't need to be a part of it. Anyway, you're a traditionally trained doctor, so you may as well stick with that, right?"

"Okay."

"You have enough going on right now. You're due in just a few days, which means it'll only get harder for you now."

"I get it, okay?"

"Plus, you insist on going to work. You don't sleep most nights…"

"How do you know?"

"I hear you in there, moving around, getting up, going to the bathroom, walking around the house."

"I'll try to be quieter."

"That's not the point. The point is that you need more sleep and rest."

"I'm eating more. Divya said I'm growing a butt."

"Finally, about two months late. But no more car trips by yourself. You know what your OB said about getting too far away from the hospital this late. I'm surprised she lets you work."

"I don't work much lately. Even if I go into labor at work, all I have to do is walk to L and D. Easy trip."

"How many work days this week?"

"Five. But just six patients in the clinic tomorrow, and only one surgical patient on Tuesday and Thursday. Easy week, for a neurosurgeon."

"And you're staying home all weekend to rest, if I have to put your foot in cement to slow you down."

"I have to make rounds on patients."

"I'll drive you and follow you everywhere you go, just so you don't get any ideas."

It wasn't far from that already, so June changed the subject. "What did you tell Auntie Haunani when I was in the bathroom?"

"Nothing you need to worry about."

June wiggled up into an upright position again, continuing to stroke her hand over her belly. "What do you mean? If it was about me, I need to know."

"Since she died before you kids were born, we were never going to bring it up."

"Bring what up?" June implored. "Who died?"

"About your grandmother, my mother."

"What about her?"

"She was a Korean comfort girl to the Japanese in the war. That's how my parents met."

That was June's next surprise of the day. "What?"

"It's not what it looks like on the surface. During the war, my father met her, took her in, tried to protect her from having to do that sort of work. Then after the war, they were on one of the first boats to America. They never said as much, but doing the math, I know I was conceived on the boat trip here."

June knew the rest of the story, of how her grandfather, a long-time heavy smoker, died of lung cancer when Mabel was a teenager. More tragically, her grandmother took her own life when Mabel was just a girl, unable to survive the scars and guilt of the war. Mabel had been the one to find her one day after school, sprawled on a bed, her wrists open to the world, most of her blood on the floor.

Still in high school, Mabel was left alone. She graduated, but just barely. She tried to get jobs, but had been shunned in post-war America. Then came the beatnik years, followed by the hippie years. In spite of hard times, she always had a place to stay with friends. Mabel didn't always know their names, but there were couches or beds to crash on for a day or two. Then she met the man she would marry. His parents took her right in, just as Amy and June came along.

"Does Amy know that about her being a comfort girl?"

"No. And she's not going to."

"As much as she nags me about being too organized and not being spontaneous, she doesn't take surprises very well, does she?" June said.

"The last thing we need to do right now is placate her. You want to know your grandmother's real name?"

"Her Korean name?" June gave it some thought. The Japanese name her grandmother had adopted on the boat to America was the only one June had known all her life.

"What was it?"

"Her family name was Kim. Her given name was Seung-ju."

"And that's why she was known as Kim?" June asked. That was the name she knew.

"She and Father thought it made her sound more American. It didn't make much difference in the end."

"I think I know enough for now. Maybe you can tell me more another time."

"We'll talk again when you're ready."

"How did Haunani get involved with that?" June asked.

"She knew there was a stain on my soul, as she called it. She knew it had something to do with my mother. When she pressed, what could I do but tell her the story?"

June felt embarrassed she didn't want to know more about her other grandmother, the one she'd never met, that had died by her own hand years before June was ever born. Even Haunani, a stranger, knew more about it than she did.

"I'm sorry if I said anything…" June began to say.

"Never mind. Some family skeletons are best left in the closet. Maybe just like Aiko?"

"Yeah. Let's leave Aiko in the closet."

"Your dimple is just like hers."

June touched her cheek. "Like your mother's? They run in the family?"

"Only on my side of the family. Same smile, too," Mabel said. "Not Amy though, just you."

"We were fashion models for many years. We have a hundred different smiles. How many women have bought some brand of lipstick only because we were smiling pretty in a magazine ad? Especially Amy."

"No, I mean your real smile."

June looked out the window at the passing scenery. "I doubt I have a real smile anymore."

"When you cry, it's the same, also," Mabel said.

"And that's why you leave me alone then?"

"You're never alone. Remember that."

They were just emerging from the tunnel, on the last leg home. June opened the window, feeling the early evening breeze blow across her face. It was soothing, at least until they got to the hospital so she could do rounds on her patients. By the time they parked next to the kitchen door at home, she was glad the day was done.

***

June made a shuffling mad dash to the bathroom as soon as they were home. She smelled something cheesy baking in the oven. June didn't care what it was, as long as there was melted cheese and garlic.

"Did Rodney get something to eat before he went back to the resort?" she asked once back in the kitchen.

"What happened to you guys?" her dad asked, looking at them both.

"Mother-daughter bonding," June said, trying to see inside the oven window.

"So sentimental these days! Where's all that sentimentality at Father's Day?"

"Inside the card Amy remembers to send you. Can we eat now?"

"And hungry all the time these days," he said. "Get plates on the table and sit down out of the way." He pulled the casserole out of the oven and carried it to the table with oven mitts.

"What is it?" June asked. She poked a fork through the thick crust of melted cheese on top, watching steam come out.

"Cheese, butter, garlic, noodles, some other stuff."

"Cheese and butter. If I'm going to clog my cranial arteries, it may as well be with cheese and butter," June said, scooping some on each of their plates.

"What did you learn from the kahuna lady?" her dad asked.

"Oh, yeah." June struggled up from her chair and went to her bedroom, returning with the rock given her by Auntie Haunani. "This is the rock she gave me to put under the crib. Nobody else is supposed to touch it at all, okay? Not even for cleaning. Okay?"

Once she pried an agreement from them to leave it alone, she put the rock under the crib that had already been set up in the corner of her bedroom.

When she got back to the kitchen, she put the leftover lumpia in the microwave and zapped them for a moment.

"Try these, Dad. They are so good."

"You got your appetite back," Tak told her.

"I can't eat enough. It's like I'm always hungry."

"Did the lady tell you anything?" he asked.

"I think she knew the baby's sex, and maybe some other things, too. Apparently, the baby is fine. Maybe that's why I'm eating so much, the baby is hungry for food now?"

"Good mood again, too," he muttered under his breath.

"Careful," Mabel said. "It doesn't last long."

"Come on, Mom."

"Hard to keep up with your moods lately. One minute you're singing to yourself, the next you're crying, then trying to bite someone's head off. Then you doze off into a nap."

"Really?"

"You napped in the car on the way to Haunani's house, you napped in the chair at the salon, and you napped again in the car on the way home. You're sleeping more during naps than you do at night."

"I do?"

Her parents shrugged at her, as if it was no secret except to her.

"Singing? When am I ever singing?"

Singing was something she never did, and something she specifically tried to avoid. Playing the car radio was as musical as she ever got and karaoke was her Kryptonite.

"Sometimes it's just humming, sometimes I hear you in the shower."

"Really?"

June gave it some thought. She was well aware of the times she had got her hooks into the people around her, but the singing was a mystery.

After dinner, Tak put the dishes in the sink to soak and wandered off to watch TV.

"Can we talk some more?" June asked when she was alone with her mother.

"What about?" Mabel sat at the table again.

"You'll think I'm nuts," she whispered when they sat on the living room couch together.

"What is it?"

"Somebody talks to me. When there's trouble. I don't mean I hear voices. It's just that a lady talks to me, gives me encouragement. "I always thought it was Grandma."

Grandma as in her father's mother, the only grandmother she had ever known.

"What brings this up?"

"Just thinking about what we were talking about in the car earlier, about your mother."

"Pardon? Today?"

"Yeah, when we talked in the car on the way home," June said.

"You mostly dozed in the car."

For the umpteenth time that day, June felt confused, but she continued on. "Well, now I think it might be your mother that talks to me sometimes."

"I'm not sure of what you mean?" Mabel said.

"Just hear me out. In the car on the way home, when you were telling me about your mother, I got sort of a creepy feeling, that maybe there was more to her than just stories I've been told."

"I still don't understand, Dear."

"It's like I have memories of her, of your mother, real memories." June wasn't sure of how to proceed, so she just jumped in with both feet. "I think she talks to me sometimes."

Mabel held June's hand. "What does she say?"

"Just that I'll be okay. To be patient." June shrugged and looked down at her hand gripping her mother's. "To struggle through to the end."

"Ha! I can see the two of you together! A couple of tragic heroes!" Mabel smiled. "But why do you think it was my mother?"

"Maybe just from what you told me on the ride home. The talk we had."

"What talk?"

"Mom, you told me all about your mother, being taken from her home in Korea to work in Japan as a comfort girl, and then coming to America on the boat."

Mabel seemed upset with what June had said. "I don't know where you heard that, but it wasn't from me. Today, you slept the entire drive home. You looked so peaceful, I didn't want to wake you up."

"I slept the whole way?" June was thoroughly confused. Maybe it was the heat the last few days, or having too much to eat, or examining the corpses in the morgue. "I could've sworn…"

"You slept most of the way to Haunani's house, at least until we got to the restaurant. Worse than that, you were out cold while waiting for me at the salon. I wish you'd start drinking some coffee again. It can't be that bad for the baby at this point."

"I slept at the salon too? How could I while the stylist used the curling iron on my hair?" June reached up to touch her hair.

"Iron? You sat in the chair and dozed."

June felt her hair, smooth and sleek, with no waves or teasing at all. "What happened? Kim did my hair."

"Kim who?" Mabel asked. "There was only one stylist there today, that young girl named Myong, and she did mine while you dozed."

"I don't understand."

"Never mind. You just need your rest. Tomorrow morning, you can have some coffee. That'll help keep you awake during the daytime so you'll sleep better at night."

"Wait. Did a woman come in acting like she knew me?"

"Kinda weird?" Mable asked. "She's the one who woke you up. She called you Aiko, you denied it, and she left."

June rubbed her face. "Something a lot more weird is going on besides her."

June went to bed early that evening, after volunteering to wash the last of the dishes. She listened to her parents in the living room, watching TV, chatting about the next day's work in the new room. The plaster on the walls would get sanded with the first layer of paint applied. Soon, the flooring would go in. With Rodney's help, real progress could be seen each day.

***

Her mother gave her a ride to work in the morning. When she got to the hospital, she breezed through the ER first, in hopes of finding nothing surgical, or at least for her. She was in her downhill slide to her delivery date, and suddenly felt very lazy.

The office manager was the first she saw when she got to her clinic.

"Doctor Kato? Your surgical case for Thursday has been cancelled."

"Oh?"

"Medical won't release him."

In a way, June was happy. The patient's primary doctor wouldn't allow surgery quite yet because of some medical issue that needed attention first. It gave her more time to relax, almost a full day off. On the other hand, the patient's surgery would be delayed a few weeks until June was back to work, or a surgeon at the other hospital might scoop him up. Either way, June didn't care much right then.

"I see. What about tomorrow's patent?"

"Still on. And I've added one appointment for this afternoon, if that's okay?"

"What is it?" Seeing another patient at the end of the day would push back her dinnertime, and she wondered why it couldn't be earlier in the day.

The office manager leaned forward across her desk and whispered, "Valley Isle Magazine wants to do a profile article on you for an upcoming issue. You're getting a good rep here already, Doctor Kato!"

"What?"

"It's okay, isn't it? It would be a lot of free publicity, plus we could use a little more fun around here."

"Yeah, it's okay, I guess." She looked at the blouse she was wearing under her white clinic jacket. It was a collarless deep crimson silk blouse she had bought recently, the last thing she had that fit around her belly without putting too much tension on the buttons. Her black knit stretch-waist pants were something better suited for winter on the mainland. "I wish I had a little more lead time, though."

"You look great. Anyway, they're running a series on the modern woman of Maui, and…"

"And I'm an example?"

"The career, the baby, your parents living with you. It's like you're living the old-fashioned values of Maui ohana but with a modern lifestyle."

"Single mothers are now considered old-fashioned?"

"Doctor, you're hot stuff on Maui."

"Ha!" June looked around to see if anyone was close enough to hear. "Did you tell them I'm a neurotic nut, flighty witch, and spend most of my spare time sitting on the toilet?'

"Maybe you can edit a few of the less important details?"

June found her first patient of the day and led him to an exam room. She had plenty of time before her next patient, so she did a slow motion neurological exam on the man, focusing on his back, and explaining the findings of the X-ray studies that had been done at the other hospital on the island. Somehow, the man had found his way to her clinic instead of going back to his first doctor.

"I have time to do your surgery later this week, but I'm afraid I might not be able to reach you by then. But you can see the problem, Mister Eisenberg. I'm due in a few days, and won't be back to work until next month."

"Not much time off."

"I have a whole schedule of patients already waiting. So, you're certainly welcome to go back to your first doctor, or wait for me."

"I already like you better. At least you're honest with me. You're sure you can't do my surgery sooner?"

"I hate to spring it on you, but what tomorrow? If I do it early enough, you might be able to go home in the afternoon. How does that sound?"

"I appreciate it, and so does my back." He smiled. "Whatever gets me back to work sooner."

She walked him out to the office manager to schedule his surgery.

June was right, though, when she told him that her surgery schedule was quickly filling for a few weeks on. She was planning to take only two weeks off after the baby came, but wanted more like two years. Still, she had to earn a living, and soon three generations of family in her little house relying on it.

She waited in her office for her next patient, talking to her old friend Becky on the phone, hearing about her adventures while on vacation. She filled the rest of her time by sending out long-overdue emails to old friends. In between emails, one showed up for her. It was from the diener at the morgue, the assistant to the pathologist. As she had requested, he did cutdowns over the stings, small slits in the skin made for further access to blood vessels, and had sent digital images of each woman's wound.

"Small punctate wounds were found in each radial artery. Upon further microscopic examination, the punctures were round, with smooth edges, as if made by a machined object, rather than the ragged appearance that would be expected from a natural sting injury."

She looked at each of the images, and sure enough they were round as though injections were given rather than ragged as if jabbed by a stinger. Next were the preliminary toxicology screen results.

Neurotoxicology results pending.

Venom Toxicology results pending.

Those were the complex tests that would need to be done in a large lab in Honolulu, on another island. "Yeah, but what about the good stuff?"

There had been varying levels of alcohol in the women's bloodstreams, not enough to cause death, but a disappointment anyway that late term women had been drinking so much.

She read further down, finding negative results for the common sedatives, hypnotics, and tranquilizers, the most common drugs used in overdoses and suicides, something she had been suspecting. Something she had considered but only fleetingly was that each woman had tried committing suicide by taking an overdose, and then purposefully allowing themselves to be stung by a scorpion they'd captured outside, believing it to be a lethal venom, just to be sure the job was done. That hadn't been the case, though. The punctures in their wrists and arteries weren't made by stingers but most likely by injection needles, something proven by the cutdowns June had asked for.

Then her eyes hit upon the one positive drug result in the lists, and the same for each victim.

"Succinylcholine?"

It was a commonly used short-acting muscle relaxant drug used in the operating room by anesthesiologists to make the passage of the breathing tube easier and safer. Its primary action was to temporarily paralyze and relax muscles by blocking nerve impulses; the downside was that the patient was unable to breathe on their own, and the drug could be used only by professionals trained in its use. The really bad part of it was, if not used with a sedative, the patient remained awake but in severe panic. They would be unable to move, breathe, or speak on their own, but be fully awake and aware of what was happening. It would be torture if not used properly.

"They had Sux in their bloodstream? What the…?"

June went back to her printed articles to read about insect and arachnid venoms. She needed a refresher course.

"That's what I thought," she mumbled, reading about the chemical components and actions of various venoms. She learned that in a very basic way, succinylcholine worked opposite to the way that venoms do: one would naturally reverse the effect of the other. "But that's not happening. What gives?"

There was a knock at her door, the signal indicating the next patient was ready for her.

After the last of her patients were gone, and the magazine interview was complete, June sat in her little office and drummed her nails. She found time during the day to swipe on some nail polish and a couple strokes of eyeliner before her interview. There were the usual kinds of interview questions she'd expect to find in a local gossip magazine: what brought you to Maui, why did you become a doctor, is it difficult to blend a career with a pregnancy and growing family. The magazine wouldn't come out for a couple of months, and by then the baby would be born, June would be back at work, and a whole new study of chaos would be taking place at home.

Tossing her white lab coat on a hanger in the bathroom, she grabbed her bag and went for a quick trip through the ER before calling for her ride home, her usual routine. She wasn't on call that evening for emergencies, but it was long a habit.

Just as she discovered nothing interesting was going on in the department, a car pulled up to the ER entrance. From inside, she watched a woman swing her door open, then race around to the back door. She looked as though she was a housekeeper of some sort, maybe from a nearby resort. She frantically began waving her arms for help.

June stood back, watching as nurses and doctors dragged a woman from the car, plunking her down on a stretcher that had been brought out. June followed the group back into the ER to watch what was going on. The woman was unconscious, arms and legs limp, her face an ominous pallor. She was also obviously very pregnant, but had no discernible injuries that June could see. It just wasn't how auto accident victims were delivered to a hospital.

The ER doctor called for the crash cart, a special cart will all the supplies and drugs needed to resuscitate an unconscious victim not breathing or with no heartbeat.

June walked over. It wasn't something for her, but she felt for the woman. Her due date couldn't have been much different from June's, a bond between them of sorts right then.

She watched as a breathing tube was slipped into her throat and hooked up to a mechanical ventilator. Nurses were busy starting IVs, giving ordered drugs, applying vital sign monitoring equipment, cutting away clothes to get access to the victim's body for further resuscitative efforts. The pregnant woman had turned into a patient as quickly as that.

The housekeeper that had brought her in stood a few feet away, nearly writing with anxiety. She was being interviewed by a nurse, and June went over to listen.

"Just on the floor, that's all! I thought maybe she was taking a nap there, but didn't open her eyes when I gave her a nudge! Then I saw that bug. Poor thing!"

June took the last step that separated them and asked a question. "There was a bug?"

"Those scorpions! Never seen them in the resort before. But there it was, squished on the floor." The housekeeper turned to look at the woman being treated. "That poor lady. I wonder where her husband is?"

"She wasn't breathing, right? And you said she has a sting on her arm?"

The housekeeper didn't answer, just shaking with fright.

June went to the stretcher where the others were furiously trying to keep the woman alive. She found an arm and looked at the wrist. It was clean. She went to the other side of the stretcher and found the deep sting mark there, right at the same spot as the women in the morgue she saw the day before: directly over the radial artery.

"Dan, this isn't a simple sting," she told the ER doctor running the show. He was one of the first people she had made friends with at the hospital. "I think it's a Sux overdose."

"What are you talking about June? She has the sting on her wrist."

"I know. But I've been looking into these recent deaths, the other stings. They've all had high levels of Sux in their systems. Plus, the punctures aren't ragged like a sting, but round as if needles had been used."

Dan looked at her, confused. "But…"

"I know what you're thinking. The choline of the Sux and the neurotoxic venin should've reversed each other. But the blood level of the Sux far out-reached the median lethal dose of whatever the scorpion stung her with."

"You think I should reverse her?"

June turned to the housekeeper again, still sniffling. "Ma'am, how long has it been since you found this lady?"

"I don't know. Ten minutes maybe?"

It had been another five to ten minutes since their arrival at the hospital, and who knows how long since the woman had been stung or injected or whatever happened before the housekeeper found her.

"Been at least twenty minutes, Dan."

"The initial effects of the Sux would've worn off. She should've been breathing on her own by now. If she had survived that length of time without breathing."

"That's what I was thinking," said June. "Try reversing the Sux anyway. Can't hurt."

That's what it often came down to in emergency medicine, try something, anything, to get a patient breathing or their heart beating again. When the usual tried and true algorithms fail, get creative.

Dan asked for the drug that would reverse the effects of the paralytic drug to be given. They watched for a while. The woman's heartbeat continued to putter along, mostly in a useful rhythm. They knew that as long as they left the breathing tube in her throat and kept her attached to the mechanical ventilator, the patient's body would get the life-supporting oxygen it needed. The bad thing was the length of time that had passed during which she hadn't been breathing.

Slowly, as the crisis settled, ER team members drifted away to other places. When June went over to see the woman more closely, she held her hand. It was warm and soft, very different from the ones she saw in the morgue the day before.

"She'll need to be admitted to the ICU," Dan said.

"I can take her on my service, if you like," June offered.

"Which is how much longer before you get a little time off, June?" he asked with a smile, looking at her belly.

She slid a hand over her tummy, feeling a kick. "Not much. But we should write this up, maybe get the other hospital involved also."

"Good luck on that front, June. The mall hospital isn't known for being friendly with us."

She was about to let go of the woman's hand when she felt a twitch. She gave it a squeeze, and thought she felt a tiny squeeze back.

"I think we have a winner, Dan."

She took the handheld exam light from the wall at the head of the stretcher and peered into the woman's eyes. Quickly doing a basic neuro function and reflex exam on the woman, they found she was getting movement back.

"I'll pass this along to the other ER docs, June, that they should try reversing an overdose of Sux if they get any scorpion sting victims."

"I bet you never thought you'd say that in your career, Dan!"

A silent hallelujah chorus went through the team still assembled. Once a hospitalist showed up, a doctor who could admit and treat the woman, June dismissed herself to home.

***

Her mother was already waiting in the pickup for her when she got out to the parking lot.

"Is it possible to run away from home on an island?" she asked after settling inside. She struggled to get the seat belt snapped.

"Only with a plane ticket. Why? What's going on?"

"I was interviewed for a magazine article today. It went okay, but I wish I could've known about it first. I just hope they do some courteous editing before it gets published." It was impossible to slouch in the large seat but she did her best. "And I have a second case to do tomorrow. Most of my day will be filled with just two cases."

"Don't you see your OB this week?"

"Wednesday afternoon. You're coming for it?" she asked.

"I promise."

"You'll be there when the baby comes?"

"I promise."

"Come on. I need more than that today. I need to know you and Dad will take care of the baby if something happens to me."

"Where's this coming from?" Mabel asked June quietly, turning the truck up their driveway and parking next to the house. They stayed in the truck to talk a while.

June sighed, slumped on the bench seat, and struggled upright again. "Another pregnant lady was brought in to the ER just a while ago."

"Is she…"

"She's okay." She told the story of the housekeeper, the sting mark in the exact same place as the others she had seen, how the patient histories were similar, all presenting in emergency rooms unable to breathe, the reason attributed to the sting and not to the undiscovered massive paralytic drug overdoses that had been administered. "Dan is going to talk to the other hospital to keep a watchful eye out for these patients and how to treat them effectively."

"Okay, problem solved. But what I want to know is how you learned all this? What have you been doing in your spare time? As if you have any spare time?"

June had to fess up that she inserted herself into investigating the deaths on her own by going to the morgue and asking questions. She got a scolding for it in return.

"How did you figure it out with just a little snooping but the county coroner here didn't?" her mother asked.

"Think about it. How many suspicious deaths does Maui get in a year? Compare that to LA, even the part of LA Mercy Hospital serves. Suspicious deaths are investigated all the time in LA, but on Maui? Can an island known for peace, quiet, and honeymoons risk exposing something like suspicious deaths? No, my money is on a coroner taking the easiest explanation possible and sweeping the details under the rug, even if it meant hiding potential murders of pregnant women."

"I can't believe a coroner would do something like that. Not in this day and age," Mabel said. "You're suggesting corruption, June."

"I don't like the idea either. But maybe when no relatives of the women came forward to insist on better explanations that poisonous stings, who cared?"

"How did you find out it was more than simple stings?"

"I insisted." June confessed about when they stopped at the hospital in town the day before, she'd gone to the morgue and she had ordered the extensive exams then. "But the thing is, that so-called birth angel has something to do with it. I just know she does."

"That woman who came into the salon and woke you up? Something was odd about her, but that doesn't make her complicit in murder."

"Why not?"

"Leave it for the police." Mabel looked at June's belly. "You've really dropped a lot, Dear."

"Yeah, and if I drop anymore, I'll need to push my belly around on skateboard." June didn't let her mother leave the pickup quite yet. "I really slept as much yesterday as you said I did? There wasn't anybody at the salon named Kim?"

"No, but don't worry about it. Late term mothers get a little whacky sometimes. Your father and I keep telling you to eat more and get more rest. That'll help even off your energy level."

"What did you mother look like, Mom? I mean around the age of thirty or so?"

"Well, that was about the age when she died. She had soft features, very feminine. Your and Amy's eyes, your dimple. Quite slender, even after she'd been in America for a while. Why?"

"Just wondering. Do you still have a picture of her? It's been since I was a kid since I've seen her picture."

Mabel dug through her purse, taking out an old black and white snapshot in a plastic case.

It was a grainy photo but June could see the resemblance between her grandmother and the stylist named Kim that had worked on her hair the day before. She gave the picture back.

"She had a high-pitched voice?"

"Yes, but all Asian women did back then. It was expected of them, sort of another way of being feminine."

"Did she learn English?"

"Once I started school. She used to study my schoolbooks in the evening. She never did get very good at it. What're all these questions, Dear?"

"Oh, just curious."

When they went into the house, June kept going through the kitchen to the bathroom. When she returned to the kitchen, dinner was already on the table.

"June, tomorrow is a short day, right? You guys want to go out to a late lunch tomorrow?" her dad asked while they ate.

"Actually, I added a case that will start late in the morning. I should be done with that at three o'clock. You guys can go and bring me back something. Might be more fun without me anyway."

"Maybe I should work on the house. If I start early and if it doesn't rain tomorrow, I might be able to get two coats of paint on, getting us one day closer to being finished. You go to the OB on Wednesday, right?" her father asked.

"It's marked on every calendar in the house, Dad, as is the scheduled delivery date, along with my clinic days and surgery days. No surprises."

She took a scoop of rice from the bucket and plunked it into her bowl. It had been a while since she had rice, another lifelong comfort food. Along with the stir-fry vegetables, she was getting her fill for dinner.

"Any scorpions in the house today?" she asked.

"Not a bug anywhere!" her dad said. "That rock must be working."

June splashed soy sauce on her rice. "I've noticed they haven't been working on the new subdivision up the hill from us lately."

"There was something in the newspaper today about some Hawaiian artifacts found further up the slope," Mabel said. "Maybe that has something to do with it."

After reading the newspaper article, she called her local source of inside information: Henry. She kept her parents at the table while she talked.

"Always finding that stuff in the islands," Henry said. "Kick over a rock and find an old fishing village. And the caves mauka are full of old bones. Once they find relics, the local people won't work there, kapu to disturb that stuff. Just like Indian burial grounds on the mainland. Impossible to get permits."

"But this is just phase one down here," June said. "The later phases are the ones that would be built further up."

"Should've had the university scientists come out to take a look before they got started," Henry said. "Probably move the whole project somewhere else."

The timing of the work stoppage was curious to June. She made another call, this one to Jack.

"When you mentioned your fear that the scorpions were coming from the construction site up the hill from you, I had someone look into the history of that part of the island," Jack said.

"Don't tell me, your social media intern, Jennifer?"

"Right. She found some old maps that indicated there had been Hawaiian villages there in the past. Your house, June, just happens to be sitting right in the middle of an ancient village. Since it's already there, no one can force you to move or demolish it, but nobody can ever do any construction on the land."

"Then you threw your weight around and gave the mayor a call to tell the land development company to knock it off?"

"No. I had Jennifer call the newspaper and tell them of our findings, making it sound like it had been a federal governmental agency discovery."

"But it wasn't. She's an unpaid intern, not a researcher," June said, wondering what kind of trouble had been drummed up with the discovery.

"Actually, she was working under a contract as a White House employee. Temporary, but government at the time of the discovery. It works, June. Air tight."

To June, it was more DC politics. "But my house is okay? I'm not going to be swarmed with inspectors and surveyors trying to scare me off my land?"

"No. And that giant pile of rocks will be bulldozed back flat again, and by the end of the week, the construction crews will be a distant memory."

"And hopefully, the scorpions will go with them."

After talking with Jack about the baby and how big she had become, June told her parents what Jack had discovered.

"Since the rock is already there, I'm leaving it," June said, thinking of the rock from Haunani that was collecting dust under the baby crib. "I don't care why they stay away, just as long as they do."

June looked down at the bowl of mint chip ice cream that had been put in front of her.

"It's a brand you can eat," her father said. "No gelatin."

"Seriously? I'm not fat enough already?" She picked up her spoon and ate the most important invention in the history of humanity.

“Nice that you have friends who can help,” her father said.

“Now if I could just get Jack to marry me, I wouldn’t have to call him every other day.”

June had her shower and went to bed right after dinner. Not that she was sleepy, she just wanted to be horizontal for the rest of the day. Sitting upright had become a chore, especially since she had dropped as her mother had said. She was able to have a text session with Amy before dozing off.

Chapter Four

"Andrea, are you with me all day?" June asked of the anesthesiologist after they had started their first case of the day. June had a spine to fix on an accident victim from several days before as her first case. She had finally convinced the hospital to buy the instrumentation, implants, and important technical equipment she needed to safely do spine surgery. In the end, June knew the hospital would benefit greatly by keeping those patients at their hospital instead of shipping them to a larger hospital on Oahu. It would take only a few months before the equipment more than paid for itself, a business side of June that the hospital was happy to have.

"First call. Here all day, until the sun comes up tomorrow, if need be."

"I won't be here that long."

Her assistant that morning was a retirement age physician who still liked to come in to feel useful. Neurosurgery was new to him, and he needed a lot of teaching, so much that she felt like she was teaching a resident again. By the time she was done with both cases that day, it would've been easier to have done them alone, and it had taken hours longer than expected.

It was almost dinnertime by the time she stepped away and pulled off her sterile surgical gown, tossing it in the trash. It didn't take long before she found a stool for a sit to read the messages she got on her phone during the case.

Just as she was reading a reminder from Divya Gill's office, her obstetrician, about the appointment the next day, and writing orders for her surgical patient, her phone rang with a call. It was an ER number.

"This is Doctor Kato," she said.

"This is Mom. I'm in the ER."

"Why are you here at the hospital?" she asked. "I didn't call for a ride home yet."

"There's bad news, Dear."

It was one of those 'oh no' moments in life. A call from a hospital emergency room with the message that there was bad news could only mean the news was worse than bad. Her blood pressure plummeted and she had to steady herself by holding on to the stainless steel counter in front of her.

"What?" was all she could spit out.

"It's your dad."

"What about him?"

"Something happened at home. I had to bring him in."

Massive panic. Nothing was more important than her parents, sister, nieces, and the baby. Jack was surrounded by security and the best medical help in the world was only steps away from him at any given moment. Everything else paled; job, house, life itself. Even if they bickered occasionally, happiness was found within the core of people orbiting around her, and nowhere else.

She pushed up from where she sat and grabbed her white doctor's jacket. She hurried to the door, trying to get the jacket around her as she walked. Her vision was narrowing, turning grayscale.

June realized then she'd been pushing her dad too hard to finish the addition on the house, making him work in the tropical heat and humidity. It was her fault he was having a heart attack, and only because she was impatient.

"What is it?" she asked going out the door in a hurry.

"Just a minute," her mother said. The call didn't end, but June couldn't hear anything going on.

She hurried as fast as she could. Tangled in the jacket half on, half off, she pulled it free and carried it in her hand.

"Mom?" she said into the phone as she hit the exit doors to the OR. "Mom!"

The ORs were on the same level as the Emergency Room, only two corners of hallways away. June was just outside the ER double doors, so she ended the call and slipped the phone into her jacket pocket.

She saw her mother at a curtained examination bay, a step up in wellness from a trauma bay. It couldn't be too bad if her father was there. Either that, or all the trauma bays were in use. Walking there as fast as she could, she saw the grin on her mother's face.

June yanked back the curtain when she got there.

"What's going on? Dad, are you okay?"

In a hospital gown, he lay on his side on the stretcher, a plain white sheet over him. There was no visible blood or bandages anywhere. He had an IV going in one arm, with a smaller piggyback slowly dripping into it. None of the gear or monitors used in cardiac resuscitation were at the bedside.

"Dad, what's wrong?"

"Your father got stung by a scorpion."

"What?"

"Hurt like the dickens, too!" Tak said. He looked unhappy, but also tried to produce a joking tone.

June went to her father's side and looked at his hand. Nothing was there.

"Where?"

"You won't see it."

"What happened, Dad?"

"He took a break from painting and sat on a rock outside to take a rest. Somebody else was already using it," her mom told her.

After glancing at all the monitors and reading the medication in the IV piggyback, she looked at her mother. "He's okay?"

"Who? Your dad or the scorpion?"

She knew then things were okay. Trying to hold back a grin, she nodded her head at her father with a silent question.

The nurse there with them explained. "Since he was wearing shorts, he barely got a jab. I doubt he got much venom. But good thing he came in here to be on the safe side. We gave him antibiotics and a tetanus shot."

"Yeah. Sore spot on both cheeks!" her dad said. "Hey, you said those things are nocturnal. What was he doing out during the daytime?"

"Probably waiting for you," Mabel said. "Had a score to settle for being swept out the door this morning."

"As soon as his IV antibiotics are in, he can go home," the nurse added.

June turned away because she had to grin. She looked back at him, smiled, and shook her head.

"You've been getting all the attention lately, Dear," her mother said. "I think he felt neglected."

"Dad, I thought you were dying in here."

"They acted like I might. I told them they never been Japanese people living in East LA."

"I bet that won a few hearts. But can you take this seriously, please? Who was your doctor?"

"Some lady doctor."

"Don't talk like that. I'm a lady doctor, too."

"Jennifer Johnson," the nurse answered.

"Hey," Tak whispered to June. "Is she any good?"

"She's as qualified as I am. Everybody here at West Maui Med is board certified and fully qualified."

"If she's as good as you, she's good enough for me."

"That's reassuring," June muttered, turning away.

June went back to the OR to write a note in her last patient's chart, and told the story of her father getting stung in the butt by a scorpion. Any other time, or any other bug, it might've been funny, but right then it concerned her. By the time she got back to the ER, they were ready to go home.

It was close to bedtime, and Tak was easily convinced to go to bed early.

"You alright, Mom?"

"He'll be okay?" she asked nervously in the kitchen.

"If he's not, the world will have a raging pregnant bitch on its hands. I'll check on him before I go to bed, just to be sure."

***

June's first job in the morning at the hospital was making rounds on her patients. She got through her morning clinic, rejoicing she had the afternoon off. She only needed to go to her OB appointment and then home for a long afternoon nap. Her mother had decided to skip June's appointment to stay with her dad all day, making June drive herself to work.

Anxious over her appointment, June skipped lunch, having only a large tumbler of ice water before going to the OB. She watched as a young woman almost as pregnant as her left the clinic, before Divya came to collect her. Two other women were waiting for appointments after June's.

"Seems like you're getting busier?" June asked to break the ice.

"Slowly but surely," the obstetrician said, showing June into an exam room. After June changed into a patient gown, she stepped up on the scale.

"Should be one forty-five," she told Divya.

Divya flicked the small weight from one side of the scale bar to the other, then pushed the larger weight one notch up.

"One fifty-one? I'm a tank!"

"Looks like we finally got to our twenty-five pound benchmark, June."

Divya did her exam, June wondering where the last few pounds came from. She decided it had to be the potatoes and ice cream her parents had been pushing on her lately.

The fetal heart tone monitor was hooked up to her belly, they listened for a few minutes, and a paper recording was taken. June kept it for a scrapbook.

"Ten more days until the big day arrives. Do you have names picked out yet?"

"Not really. I think we've settled on Logan or Melanie, but nothing firm yet. Hard to decide since I don't know the sex."

Divya brought the ultrasound machine over, warmed the gel, and squirted some on June's belly.

"Want to know?"

"Maybe I should." June bit her lip. She felt a little like a naughty schoolgirl, trading gossipy secrets with a pal. "Yeah, show me. But promise not to tell the others you told me, okay?"

Divya turned the ultrasound monitor so June could watch. With just a little pressure from Divya's ultrasound wand on one side of her belly, June could see right away what gender of baby was coming. She rested her head back and began sorting through dozens of names she had been considering, throwing out half of them.

"Your baby is doing a headstand on your bladder, June. That's why you have no capacity these days."

"That means it's soon, right? With the head in that position?"

"Not necessarily. Primips can lighten like this for quite a while, much longer than multips. But you still need to be careful." She put the ultrasound away. "What's your schedule like for this week? Are you busy in the OR?"

"My only case for tomorrow cancelled, and Friday's clinic schedule is light, just two people in the morning. Next week, I've purposefully scheduled nothing for the OR, and just mornings in the clinic. By then, I think I'll be way too distracted to focus on much of anything."

"Next week, you'll need to stay close to home. Only back and forth to the hospital and home, nowhere else, okay? Even this weekend. You're a lady of leisure for now on during this pregnancy. Doctor's orders, so enjoy it!"

Divya told her the story of one woman that went for a hike on a popular trail upcountry the day before her due date, ending up delivering that same day.

"I have Miller lined up to do my epidural. He's on call the day I'm due," June mentioned, after hearing the story and getting another stern warning.

"I heard. He does a nice job of epidurals. But you know, babies have a schedule of their own."

"I'm not giving birth to a misbehaving baby."

"Who's your pediatrician?"

"Peterson, if I can convince him to come in from the golf course."

"Okay, fine," the obstetrician said. "Is there anything else? Any questions?"

June struggled into her clothes, the tiny Divya helping.

"The baby is okay, right? Everything is on track?"

"Everything is perfect. For almost nine months, you've been the perfect mother."

"Yeah, but…"

"And you will continue to be the perfect mother." She gave June's arm a squeeze. "You've done everything right. Now just stop worrying and enjoy these last few days, okay? Let your parents dote over you."

"I'm not so sure about my parents. Dad got stung in the butt by a scorpion and Mom is getting forgetful. They have someone helping with the addition, trying to get it done before the baby comes, but he goes home in a couple more days."

"I heard about the room. Sounds ambitious."

"For them, a crossword puzzle is ambitious," June said, walking with Divya down the hall to the waiting room.

***

For the first time in several days, Becky and her boyfriend Kyle came by with Rodney for breakfast. It was good to have so many young people in the house then, and to hear about the adventures they were going on. Rodney was officially done with his work on the new addition, and was paid just before they left.

"How's your butt, Dad?" she asked once they had the time to themselves.

"Butt's fine. The sting hurts like the dickens." He rubbed back there for show. "Better than yesterday, anyway. Maybe those guys know what they're doing at your hospital."

"Imagine that," June said. "What's everyone doing today?" June asked, pushing her oatmeal around with a spoon. It was her second breakfast of the morning, trying to feed the baby what it was demanding. She felt huge, even bigger than the day before, and the baby was kicking a lot more than usual. "I don't want you working on the house yet."

"Day off for you, too. You're going back to bed and get more rest," Tak told her in the commanding voice he rarely used.

"I've been in bed for the last twelve hours!"

"I want the new room done and usable before the baby gets here. Big push on that the next few days," her father said, plunking fresh chunked papaya in June's oatmeal. "Your mom has errands to do, some organic farmer's market upcountry she heard about."

"Kula, wherever that is," Mabel said.

June pushed away her empty bowl, now full. "Don't get lost."

"It's an island," Mabel said. "Can't get lost."

"I'm taking the pickup to the big hardware store in town to get a few things. Linoleum flooring today. Sink, tub, and toilet going in soon."

"You're sure you can work with your sting? Or even sit on it long enough to drive to town?"

"I saw it this morning," Mabel said. "It's just a bruise."

"Strong as ever," he said.

"I bet," June said. She knew what they meant by being 'strong'. From what she heard early that morning coming from their bedroom, he wasn't suffering much from his sting. "How do you stick the floor down?"

"Glue."

"Does it stink?"

"Yeah," her dad said quietly. He pushed her breakfast bowl back in front of her. "But only for a few hours."

"No chemicals around the baby, remember?"

"Maybe we can tape up plastic sheeting and vent it outside with fans?" he said.

When the baby went into a kicking frenzy, June interpreted it as being hungry. She stabbed a piece of her papaya and took a bite. "When you get back, you need to put the funnels on the legs of the crib, remember?"

"Need some duct tape also. I'm going to wrap the legs of the crib with duct tape, with the sticky side facing out," her dad said. "But perfect time for you to lie in bed like queen for a day."

"More like a beached whale."

"That's okay too," her mother said. "Pretty soon, back to *takenotsue*." Bamboo stick.

"Yeah, that's right!"

"Tawameru demo kudaku-nai!" the three Katos said together, as though 'bend but never break' was a family motto. Bamboo was famous for bending in the wind but not breaking, giving it the reputation of being strong.

"Maybe you should get a room at the hotel across the street for the night while the glue dries?" her mother offered.

"I could use the air conditioning, and some peace and quiet."

"We're not noisy," her father said.

June considered bringing up the noise she heard that morning but let it go. "No, you're not. But sometimes I'd just like to be alone. And I know you guys would rather not have me around for a while. I'll look for a room later."

One by one, they drifted off to prepare for their days, leaving her alone at the breakfast table.

The dishes were left behind for June, her one and only task to accomplish that day while the others were out. She waved from the back door as her dad went off in the truck, and Mabel in the car with her map, yellow highlighted markings for the route she was supposed to take, and the admonition that if she got lost to call home.

June did the dishes and cleaned the kitchen. After her shower, she leaned over to look at the rock still under the crib where she had put it, getting a strong kick from the baby for her efforts.

In the quiet house, lying on the bed, she was instantly bored. She got her phone and sent a few texts out, not hearing from anyone in return, even Amy. A half-read romance novel beckoned to her, but not enough for her to get off the bed to go get it. Instead, she reached for the medical journals and articles stacked on her nightstand, and grabbed the informational booklet for all professional licensing in the state, something she requested when she first moved to Hawaii and became licensed as a physician.

"Hawaii State Licensing Division," she said to herself. She pushed a pillow behind her back to prop herself up, shoved a flat pillow between her legs, and pounded the pillow flat under her head. "Let's see if birth angels need licenses to work here."

She looked for any licensure similar in name to 'birth angel' but found nothing. She tried 'doula' next, read the short explanation for it, and saw that certification existed.

Feeling as bold as she was curious, she called the main office in Honolulu for professional licensing. She explained she was a doctor on Maui, implied she was an obstetrician, and that she was considering hiring someone for her office.

The clerk searched for the name 'Marilyn Scanlon' while remaining on the phone with June.

"Zero results, Ma'am. I tried simply 'Scanlon'. Still zero."

"Okay, so she's not a doula. Let's try midwife."

The clerk found nothing listed for that also.

"Is there any way to search all professional licensing records?" June asked.

After being put on hold for a moment, the clerk came back on the line.

"She's had Registered Nurse licensure in the State of Hawaii."

"What? She's a nurse?"

"Was. Her license has been terminated."

"Terminated? What's that mean?"

"Our records indicate voluntary surrender of licensure."

"So, she *was* a nurse, but not a midwife, and voluntarily gave up her license for some reason. There has got to be a story in there somewhere."

"I don't know, Ma'am. Is there anything else?"

"Is there any indication of where she worked? Or a specialty?"

"I have no indication of that. We don't have employment records here."

"Try searching for the first name of Katrina, in nurses, doulas, midwifes, the works. Is that possible?"

"It's a fairly unusual name." She heard the clerk sigh. "I'll have to call you back."

"Okay, but first, look to see if there are any licensing or certification requirements for something called a 'birth angel'."

"Not that I can find, Ma'am."

June ended the call to let the clerk do the search she had requested. "So, the scam artist birth angel sends patients…no, let's call them clients…to a therapist with no qualifications. Isn't that a tidy little arrangement?" she said quietly in the room. "And they're trying to open a colony of women and babies. How is this not a cult? It's not like a hippie commune where everybody lived for free and helped each other do whatever it was they did on hippie communes. These are affluent young women living in condos in a Maui resort area. Somebody other than the realtors is benefitting from this deal."

It wasn't long before her phone rang with a return call from the clerk. "I cross referenced the name Katrina with those licensures you requested and found nothing even remotely similar. Is there anything else I can help you with?"

"No, I guess that wraps it up."

For some reason, the information that Marilyn Scanlon was truly a scam artist, just as June had expected all along, put her in a good mood. It also meant she was that much closer to exposing something very sinister occurring on the island.

The sun was beginning to shine through the wooden slatted blinds left half open. Beginning to shine on her legs, June kicked off the sheet, leaving her naked but for her stretched tank top and undies. Journals, papers, the phone book, and notes were scattered all over the bed in a mess, not much different from when she was in college studying for an exam. So far, it had been a productive morning, in spite of the soccer match being waged in her belly.

She wondered who else she could call to ask a few questions that wouldn't raise suspicion. She knew no one at the mall hospital, and the only obstetrician she knew personally was Divya, her own. If she called her, it would raise too many unwanted questions. She poked around her phone numbers and found the one she wanted.

"Dan, June Kato. Are you busy?" It was the doctor in the ER that had treated the emergency scorpion sting victim from the resort the day before.

"Hanging out. Just sent someone in for an appy. Why? Are you okay?"

"I'm fine. But I'm home alone on a day off and I'm bored out of my mind. You know any of the OBs at the other hospital?"

"You sure you're okay?"

"I'm fine, Dan. I just saw Divya yesterday and everything is fine. But I met this lady the other day, and I'm a little curious about her. I think maybe she worked over at the other hospital as a nurse a while back."

"Does she work at West Maui Med now?" Dan asked.

"Not that I'm aware of. She might've been an OB nurse for a while. Do you know anybody over there you could ask?"

She gave him Marilyn's name and let him make some calls. While she waited for him to call back, she read a return text from Amy asking for a picture of her tummy, which she took and sent, along with the message of *25#*. Instead of getting a text, Amy called.

"You're so big, Babe. Did you go to your OB yesterday?"

"I've gained seven pounds in the last week. But I think most of it is in my ankles. Mom says I've dropped a lot."

"It wasn't long after I dropped that the girls came, remember? What did the OB tell you?"

"Nothing. Everything is fine. Perfect position. Baby is doing a head stand on my bladder."

"And you're scheduled for a week and a half from now?"

"Ten days. Running out of time. And you know what? I'm finally starting to enjoy this. I have no cases scheduled for the OR, and a light schedule in the clinic next week. I really don't have to go anywhere until after the weekend except to do rounds. Mom and Dad are doting over me. None of my clothes fit, even the pregnancy stuff, so I spend most of my time in baggy shorts and old T-shirts. If I get any bigger, I'll need to get something tailor-made at Maui Tent and Awning."

"I'm coming."

"No, just stay home. You guys are too busy."

"I can leave the girls with Mick. They can bond. A little self-supervision will do them some good."

June could argue as easily as Amy. "Mom and Dad can watch over me."

"And if the baby comes in the middle of the night, they're getting out of bed to take you in?"

"The hospital is a mile away. I can drive myself if it comes to that."

"What? I'm not letting you drive yourself to the hospital while in labor. They don't know how to handle you. When was the last time they did anything as important as this?"

"I'm just having a baby, Sis."

"Oh, listen to this! Just having a baby!"

June wasn't sure how it was left, if her sister was coming for the birth or not. She had wanted to ask her to, to beg her to come for months, but also knew Amy was too busy with her fashion clothing company, twin seven-year-olds, and a new husband of her own. Deep down inside, though, she wanted her there when the time came as much as anybody else, maybe even as much as she wanted Jack to be there.

Spinning her phone in circles on the bed sheet, it rang.

"June, I called an OB I surf with occasionally and asked him about that name. He remembered her pretty well. She was a nurse in maternity at the hospital until a couple of years ago."

"I see. Did he say anything else about her?"

"Only that she was bad news warmed over. Not only did the hospital fire her, they contacted the licensure division to complain."

June struggled to a sitting position. "What for?"

"Working outside the scope of her licensed practice."

"No way! What was she doing?"

"Crazy stuff. Blessings, massages with stones. She held a séance in a Filipina patient's room once, and apparently scared the poor girl half to death."

A weird massage and stones sounded familiar.

"But that's not enough to lose a license, is it?"

"She was also caught diverting meds."

"Stealing patient meds? Now that's just plain wrong. Someone needed to take her out back and..."

"June, however you know that woman, it's best you stay far away. She sounds like bad news in a can."

***

"What do you think, Baby?" June asked, rubbing her hands over her round belly in circular motions.

She got a solid kick.

"That's what I think too."

At first, June considered calling Detective Atkins back to have a talk with him. Figuring he would have no more interest today than he had earlier, she gave up on him. She found a non-emergency number for the police department in the phone book and called.

"Yeah, hi. I'd like to know how to report a crime."

"This line is for business and non-emergency calls, Ma'am. You should hang up and call Nine-One-One immediately if a crime has been committed."

"No, well, you see, I think a crime has been committed, but don't really have concrete proof. Not really an emergency."

She heard a sigh. "And the crime, Ma'am?"

"Murder."

"Ma'am?"

"I think someone is killing pregnant women on the island."

She went on to explain her thoughts and suspicions. In the end, the officer on the phone gave her the location of the main police department on the island for her to give a formal report.

"Once you give a report, detectives would have to investigate."

"All the way in to Kahului to give a report? Someone can't come out to me?"

"Just near the shopping mall. Easy to find."

He hung up on her. June figured she was being laughed at in the precinct house over her suspicions of scorpions being used to murder pregnant women.

She was supposed to stay home and rest that day. Anyway, she'd have to take a taxi from one part of the island to another, paying a huge fare, just to make a report that might never get looked at. She also thought it was odd he called it a report rather than a witness statement, or simply just a statement. Thinking about the details she would have to give, June knew she would sound like a crackpot pregnant woman to the police.

"You see, it's like this," she said, pretending to talk with a cop. "There's this lady in a caftan with a shaved head that reads fortunes and massages auras, going around killing pregnant women with a powerful drug found only in hospitals. And then she stings them with a scorpion at the same time, just to cover up her crime." She stopped rubbing her belly. "Yeah, that wouldn't sound insane at all."

She wanted to do some primping while thinking about how to proceed with the police. June looked at her fingernails and tried filing them. Her toenails were long overdue for attention, a place she hadn't been able to comfortably reach for weeks. Looking in her one and only bottle of nail polish, it was dry. Her brows were in order, she didn't have the patience for a facial, and after her recent minor psychotic event at the salon, she was going to leave her hair alone. About all she could do was take a shower.

There had already been a lot of clamor in her abdomen that day, even more than usual. June chalked it up to the baby being fed only twice so far that day. She found a piece of leftover toast in the kitchen and washed it down with half a cup of leftover cold coffee, her first in several days.

"There. You're now officially addicted to caffeine, Baby," she said, stroking both hands in circles over her tummy, trying to calm the baby.

After one last bite of cold toast, she found a business card in her clutch and called the number for Myong's salon.

"Do you do nails there?"

"Yeah! No appointment, just come in anytime."

That gave her two reasons to shower and make the trip into town. Going to the police and getting her nails done was all she needed as incentive for cracking out of her prison for a while. She had been abandoned by everyone at home, she was more than caught up on her sleep, and the baby had been fed three times. Now, she had places to go, people to see, and real reasons for it. If she hurried, she could be back home before her family discovered she'd been out.

"Those guys won't be back until later this afternoon. If I do this right, I won't get a scolding."

She poked through her closet for something that might fit. There was a peachy knitted but thin sleeveless cashmere sweater that covered her to the waist. Digging through her father's dresser drawers, she found some of his nicer shorts. They were dark blue, which didn't go with her top, but at least they fit around her hips.

"So much for fashion," she muttered. "A peach sweater and men's shorts for clothes, a moon face, and daikon legs. If those old cosmetics advertisers could see me now!"

She called a local cab company, someone that served the area resorts with airport services. It was only a few minutes later that she was stretched out on a seat of a van big enough for several people and their luggage, only a clutch in her hand, the A/C blowing in her direction.

"Going to the airport?" the young man with a shaggy surfer haircut asked. He had a mainland accent.

"No. Police Station in Kahului."

Even though the baby was quiet, June was hungry again, or at least felt something like hunger pangs. Once the baby became busy, it wasn't a soccer game or kickboxing, but more of somersaults. More food should quiet it, but she had a reason to go somewhere besides work, and someone to take her there that wouldn't give her a lecture about taking risks while pregnant. Another meal could wait.

After the half-hour ride, the driver pulled the van into the police station parking lot.

"How much to wait a few minutes?" June asked from her seat.

"Seventy-eight dollars already."

"What?"

"Taxis are an expensive way to go places on Maui. Should've asked me to take you to the airport with some other passengers. That's only fifty bucks from West Maui resorts."

"Just wait about ten minutes."

She struggled out, barely getting her feet to the ground without falling, the driver watching the whole time. Inside the police station, she was the only citizen there wanting to do business. She got a report form, filled it out, and with very little pomp or circumstance, handed it over to the officer manning the desk.

"Someone will actually see that?" she asked.

"It'll be scanned by the desk sergeant before being sent to the appropriate division."

Police lingo sounded the same the world over. "But someone will eventually see it?"

"We receive many citizen complaints every week. They all get read and prioritized."

It was police lingo for 'get lost'. She'd heard it before. "Yeah, thanks."

Leaving the precinct, she climbed back into the van.

"Back home again?"

"Main Street in Wailuku."

If she was coming all the way to town and spending close to a hundred bucks for the ride, she was getting something out of it. Twenty nails were going to get the deepest red color Myong had to paint on them.

Getting to the next stop, she begrudgingly paid him a hundred dollar bill and kept her hand out for the change, leaving him without a tip.

"Hey!" he shouted, and held out his hand once she was safely outside the van and on the ground. "I waited for you!"

June pointed at her belly. "Should've been a gentleman and helped the pregnant lady out of the van."

She only needed to go half a block to Myong's salon, her first stop, to get her nails done. Further on was a trendy women's clothing store, but new clothes could wait. Meaningless gossip and chatter from Myong sounded more inviting right then. She might even get to the bottom of her fantasy of meeting someone named Kim, or hallucination. Anyway, she felt a few more spasms from not eating much for breakfast, and the baby was beginning to kick again. She needed to at least sit down.

When she got to the salon, a client was being attended to, and two more women were waiting in chairs at the front. Instead of going in to wait, she headed down the block to the coffee shop for something to drink and maybe a pastry to feed the baby.

The hot weather of the last few days had broken, the tradewinds had returned, and Maui was once again blessed with a comfortable morning. She felt great as she waddled along, her belly sitting low, able to breathe deeply the clean Hawaiian air.

Between Myong's salon and the coffee shop was Pandora's Health Clinic, where Marilyn Scanlon worked. June had half a mind to go in and tell her off about being a fraud and practicing quackery, something she still planned to write letters about to the state and possibly even the newspapers.

"Somehow that woman needs to be exposed," she muttered as she walked along, looking in shop windows.

She got up to Marilyn's little clinic, and saw a light on inside. When she drew up to the door, she could see Marilyn sitting behind her desk, cheerfully waving her in.

"Forget you," June muttered. She kept going.

"Aiko?"

June's shoulders slumped.

"Aiko? Why don't you come in? I can do a free aura massage!"

June turned back but held her ground. "Free baloney, isn't it?" She didn't try hiding her natural voice.

Marilyn's face suddenly changed. "Pardon? Maybe you should come in for a rest. Come in out of the hot sun."

June closed the distance between them. "It's not hot and don't tell me what to do."

"What's wrong? I thought we were friends, you and me?"

Marilyn held the door open to her little clinic. She was wearing a different caftan that day, but just as billowy. A strand of heavy plastic beads hung from around her neck.

June had a hard time controlling her voice. "One thing we're not is friends!"

A couple of other people stopped to watch, June barely noticing them.

"Just come inside and we'll talk." Marilyn pushed the door further open.

June noticed the others nearby looking at her, and not wanting to make a scene in public, stepped inside. If she was going to make a fool of herself with a shouting match, it may as well be inside in relative privacy.

"I'm on to you, Marilyn. I know you were fired from your job as a nurse and lost your license. I also know there's something very odd about some of your so-called clients, about how a few of them have died recently."

"Come on in the exam room where we can be comfortable," Marilyn said, trying to lead June into the back area of the clinic.

June wasn't going any further. She would have her say and leave.

"I know your clients have had succinylcholine injected into their radial arteries, and right through scorpion stings as though you were trying to hide it."

"Arteries? Sucks what?" Marilyn feigned ignorance, but June wasn't buying it.

"I've heard all about your past. You were an OB nurse at the hospital and got caught diverting drugs from patients. I bet it was Sux, wasn't it? And who better to know where to inject a bolus of drug that would travel right to the heart and brain than a nurse? How many women have you killed, making it look like a scorpion sting, or centipede bites, or whatever the heck you've used?"

"What do you know about anything?" Marilyn demanded. "You don't know what you're talking about! You don't even know your own name! You're a raving lunatic!"

"I know you're an insult to the nursing profession!"

Marilyn looked at the front window. June glanced and saw a small crowd had formed. Marilyn dropped the louvered blinds and closed them. She locked the door and threw the deadbolt.

"Trying to hide?" June demanded. "Hide in here all you want, but I've already filed a police report. Otherwise, good riddance to you!"

While June worked with the locks, trying to get the front door open, Marilyn went to the back room and emerged a moment later, a drug vial and syringe in her hands. She was hurriedly drawing up a full syringe.

"What's that? Your stash of drugs?" June demanded when she looked back at her. The deadbolt was stiff to work, and June couldn't quite get it undone.

"Those women didn't know what they were doing! They could've had peaceful, wondrous events, but they ruined it for themselves! They didn't believe in my work, in the Goddess in their souls!"

June was instantly pissed. She had heard enough about goddesses, peace, and wondrous events from Marilyn. She was also beyond caring about making a scene in public. Her temper was up, and so was the baby, kicking madly then.

She automatically put her hand on her belly, stroking it to quiet the baby. It wasn't helping. "So, you killed them because they didn't believe in your fraudulent maternity care?" she yelled. "You killed five women, just because they didn't buy into your baloney?"

"And now it's your turn!"

Marilyn lunged at June, leading with the syringe. As quick as Marilyn lunged, June dropped her clutch, sidestepped, and grabbed the arm holding the syringe. Marilyn gave June a hard bump in the belly when they met.

June hadn't got much exercise lately, and was overpowered by the larger Marilyn. She felt the sting of something on her skin near her shoulder, but pushed away. With the jab in her skin, the baby gave one big kick.

Marilyn came at her again, but June was ready with her favorite boxing combination, learned in advanced self-defense classes, and practiced many times since. Her hands balled into fists, she threw a left jab at Marilyn's face, followed by a second. Oddly, they barely slowed Marilyn down. June tried a right cross, but with her belly so big, wasn't able to turn and put power into it. She was successful at giving her a good jolt, the syringe flying away from Marilyn's hands.

There was a hammering knock at the front door, followed by pounding on the front window. June heard a familiar voice yelling outside. Before June could scream for help, Marilyn shoved June, making her stumble back, slamming into a wall behind her.

That's when she felt the flood of warm water down her legs. She touched the shorts she was wearing, and looked at her fingertips.

"You broke my water!"

Marilyn said nothing, but came at June with the syringe again. June didn't hold back; there was no reason to. She had a baby coming and survival was all that mattered.

She threw possibly the hardest right cross she'd ever thrown, connecting with Marilyn's jaw, sending the woman reeling backwards. She landed flat on her back and remained motionless, her strand of beads lying across her face.

June heard a siren, and hoped it was for her. She went to the door and finally got the locks open. She felt unsteady, and the baby was kicking up a storm.

When she looked outside at the crowd that had gathered, she saw a familiar face right at the front.

"Kim?"

Kim rushed through the door and pushed June to a chair. "What's going on? Did she hurt you?"

"My water broke."

Kim looked down at the fluid on the floor.

"You need the hospital!"

June began rocking in her chair, clutching her belly, trying to support it. A sweat had broken out and a spasm jolted her. She knew then that what she thought all morning were hunger pangs and tumbling demonstrations had been early labor pains. She saw the look of concern on Kim's face. Right then, the hairstylist was her best friend, and was a real person after all.

A cop rushed in, his pistol drawn.

"I think I'm in labor. Can you call me an ambulance?" June asked him.

"What happened?" he asked, going to the unconscious Marilyn on the floor.

Kim gave the explanation, pointing at Marilyn. "Big fight! That weirdo tried to hurt my friend!"

The cop didn't pay any attention to the excited Kim, so June took over explaining.

"She tried to inject me with a drug that would paralyze me," June explained, still rocking through another labor contraction. Pointing to the syringe, she went on to give a quick story about Marilyn, and the scorpion stings. "I just made a report at the police station a little while ago."

Two more cops showed up. "Cuff her," the first officer at the scene said, pointing to Marilyn, who had come around and was sitting up. "First charge, aggravated assault, attempted murder."

"My contractions are really close together. Am I getting an ambulance soon?" June stayed in her chair, Kim sitting next to her, stroking her hand. When the cops began to discuss what to do with Marilyn, and another tried checking on the ambulance, June looked at Kim. "You should get back to work, Kim. Myong will be wondering what happened to you."

"And leave you alone? No way."

June watched as the police officer talked on his phone, until he hung up. "Big accident upcountry. Too many ambulances up there right now. I'll have to take you."

"Where? Upcountry? What part?"

"I'm not sure. Maybe Kula side."

"Kula?" June asked. "How many ways are there to get to Kula?"

"Not many," the officer said.

It was the second heart-sinking 'oh no' moment in the last few days. Before, it was her dad at the hospital. Today, it was a big accident right where her mother went driving alone.

"Can you find out something about the accident?" June asked, trying not to yell. "Like who was hurt? How many people were involved?"

"You want go to hospital, or you want traffic reports?" the officer asked. He helped her stand, June unable to get upright, another wave of contractions hitting her, Kim supporting her other side.

"Kim, get my clutch."

"You already have it in your hand."

Confused, June shoved her little wallet into her pocket while being led out of the door by the cop. Kim joined them, helping June into the police car. Several bystanders watched as Marilyn was pushed into another police car.

It was the typical squad car, with the back seat removed and the interior vinyl-coated for easy cleaning. It smelled musty, maybe with the hint of old vomit. But right then, June didn't care about smells. She only wanted the contractions to slow down.

With the cop driving, lights and siren blaring, Kim tried comforting June in the back of the squad car. June couldn't help but sprawl. She looked out the window when she felt the car make a hard turn.

"Where are you taking me?" she asked.

"Hospital, right over here," he told her.

"No!" June doubled over with another contraction. "No, my OB is at the other hospital in West Maui."

"Good guys over here, too," he said, looking at her in the mirror.

"You have time," Kim told her. The sound of her voice was soothing, the sound of family in it. She looked at Kim, getting a reassuring smile in return.

"I have to go to the other one, please," June begged. "It'll be okay."

He slowed to make a hard U-turn.

With another contraction, June wondered how dilated she was. Things were going quickly, much faster than what she'd read or how Divya had taught her it would go. Even with lights and sirens blaring from the police car, the trip to the other hospital would take at least a half hour. Another contraction hit. She counted the seconds before the next contraction. “Officer, you might want to snap it up.”

She took out her phone and dialed. She listened as it rang eight times, ten, twelve, fifteen. In her excited confusion, she tried to remember her OB’s clinic and surgical schedule. The call finally went to voice mail, and she left the message for Divya to call her.

“Come on, where are you, Divya. Please don’t be in the middle of surgery.”

She suffered another wave of contractions, and looked at her watch. They were too close together.

“Breathe, Honey,” Kim told her. She hadn’t noticed before, but Kim was wiping sweat from June’s face. “Just calm down and breathe quiet.”

“Okay.” She couldn’t.

She called Divya’s office, but that call also went to voice mail. It was lunchtime at the hospital, apparently not a good time for baby emergencies.

Dispatcher calls were coming over the police radio in the car, and the cop turned it down a little. There was noise from the car’s siren, and the occasional screech of tires on asphalt.

June dialed another number, one she hated to call right then, her mother’s. It too rang, four times, six, eight times.

Tears began to stream down her face, Kim trying to wipe them away, June ignoring her efforts. She tried Divya’s personal cell phone number, but it went to voice mail again.

“Where is everybody?”

June looked out the window at the scenery, but it didn’t register. Nothing was registering except labor pains, contractions that were too close together, her obstetrician not answering her phone, and her mother right in the middle of a big accident. It was so big, in fact, there were no available ambulances to take her to the hospital.

This wasn't how she planned having her baby.

She tried her father's phone, but got no answer, not so unusual since he left it off most of the time. She tried her mother's number again, and began to panic when it still wasn't being answered. She decided to let it ring until someone answered. There was nothing else she could do.

Finally, it was answered on the umpteenth ring.

"Mom! Are you okay? I heard about a big accident where you are!"

No one spoke from the other end of the call.

"Mom? Mom!"

She put the call on speaker so she wouldn't have to hold the phone to her head.

"Is that what it is? Big traffic jam, so I turned around again. But I'm not sure how to get home."

June heaved a sigh of relief. "Mom, you're alright?"

"Yeah. Why?" her mother asked back. "I might be late getting home. The main road up here is blocked off and now I'm a little lost. I might have to drive all the way around the island to get home again."

"She's upcountry?" the cop asked.

"Kula."

"Tell her to find a road that goes downhill. Any road. Then turn toward the ocean. When she gets there, turn right. She can't get lost that way."

"What's going on, Dear? What's all the noise? Aren't you at home?"

"I'm in labor, Mom. My water broke and I'm having contractions."

"Don't worry. First time for you. Labor takes a long time for first timers."

"Except it took only an hour for Amy. And you've said it wasn't long for you either." June struggled with a flash of a contraction. "Anyway, I'm already dilating."

"How do you know?"

June squinted through a hard contraction, gripping Kim's arm tightly. With a sigh at the end, she said, "I'm a doctor, remember? They teach these kinds of things in medical school."

She felt a rumbling, then another contraction hit. Kim stroked her head, cooing to her to relax.

"You're a doctor?" the cop said over the noise of his siren.

"Uh huh," was all June could say to him. She picked up the phone to talk to her mother. "Just drive safe and go straight to the hospital, okay?"

Kim told her to slow her breathing, to stop the panting June had started. She tried Divya's phone again, still with no answer. With Kim cooing her nerves down and wiping sweat from her face, June called the last number she could.

"Sis…"

"Hey, what's up? What's all the noise?"

"I'm in a police car, going to the hospital."

"What?"

"My water broke. My contractions are really close together. That's good, right?"

"If you're in the dang hospital, it's great! But it sucks if you're in the back of a police car! Is anybody with you?"

June kept rocking, accepting the comfort from Kim, listening to traffic as the police car rushed down the highway, the siren blaring. "Kim's here."

"Who in the world is Kim?"

"My new best friend. Can you try calling Dad? He went out…" A new wave of contractions hit her, which she suffered through by shoving her feet up against the car door and pushing. "He went out to find a toilet…but he's not answering his phone."

"Looking for a toilet? What's going on there, Babe?"

"Chaos."

"Make sense, will you?" Amy demanded.

"He went shopping…for stuff for…the bathroom…"

"Why is he out shopping if you're in labor?"

"Never mind that. Just keep calling Dad and send him to the hospital."

She handed the phone to Kim to put in her pocket, just before another contraction. They had already sped through the tunnel several minutes before and June knew she wasn't far from the hospital. She listened as the officer called ahead to the Emergency Room about their impending arrival.

"Contractions coming fast now, but don't push," Kim told her. She pushed June's feet off the car door. "Don't push."

"The baby's coming," June whined. "She's coming."

June panted through a long, steady contraction, the way she had learned in classes. But she didn't have her OB there, or her mother and birth coach with her, but instead a hairstylist she barely knew. More than anything, she wanted her epidural before it was too late.

She felt inside her shorts.

"I need my phone, Kim."

"Just breathe slow…"

"My phone!"

She tried Divya's office again, now that they were close.

When someone answered, June tried not to yell. "Yeah, this is June Kato, a patient of Doctor Gill. Is she there? I really need to talk to her."

"She's over at the other hospital today, but she should be done soon. Can I send her a message?"

"Just my luck. Tell her I'm crowning, and if she doesn't get to the hospital in the next few minutes, she'll miss all the fun. Who's on call today?"

"Doctor Wilson, but I know he's very busy with patients of his own in L and D."

June gave the phone back to Kim, just as the officer pulled into the Emergency Room loading area. He brought nurses out with a stretcher. In a flash, they had June in a trauma bay, the curtains pulled around her for privacy. A nurse propped her head up, and June naturally bent her knees.

"I need to go to Labor and Delivery! Not here!"

"No rooms there. Not even doctors or nurses available right now. You're going to have to relax and hold on," a nurse told her.

"Relax? Find Doctor Peterson. He's my pediatrician."

"Not even pediatricians available right now."

A nurse tugged at June's cashmere sweater, trying to get it off, but June wasn't complying, focused more on breathing and clamping her teeth together. In the rush to the hospital, she'd broken into a heavy sweat. Her sweater was soaked and her hair wet with perspiration stuck to her face. Vital sign monitors were quickly being applied, the blood pressure cuff, EKG patches, all the usual for any emergency patient.

She tried swatting hands away. “I don’t need that! I’m having a baby, not a heart attack!”

“Standard operating procedure for all ER patients, Ma’am.”

“Don’t call me Ma’am. Is there a doc around? Is Dan here?” June asked once the frazzled energy around her had settled. “What about an anesthesiologist?”

“Oh, you’re way past getting an epidural!” one of the nurses said with a chuckle.

“Dan’s with a heart attack patient right now,” another nurse said.

Her wet shorts were pulled away and she finally consented to have her top removed, before being helped into a hospital gown. More contractions hit just as a fetal heart rate monitor was strapped around her.

“I should look,” the nurse said, snapping gloves onto her hands.

“I’ve been crowning for a while now.”

The nurse pulled back the thin sheet over June and checked. “Wow! You sure are!”

June suddenly remembered the abandoned Kim, waiting somewhere.

“Kim!” she called out from behind the curtain.

Kim poked her head in.

“Sorry about all this, but maybe you can get a ride back to town with the cop?”

“I can wait until your mother gets here. I’d like to see her again.”

In the midst of the heaviest and longest contraction yet, she heard her father’s voice. The curtain got yanked back.

"What's going on? Amy called and said to come here right away!" he said, going to June's side.

"Sorry, Dad. I should've listened to you and stayed home." June interrupted her panting. "Any minute…"

"You're here at the hospital. That's what matters."

"Have you seen Mom?" June asked through more panting.

"She was just coming in the parking lot. Where's Doctor Gill?" he asked.

June was soaked in sweat by that time, and had a hard time gripping the hands of a nurse and her father through the next contraction, following on the heels of the previous. "On her way…" she said with her eyes clamped shut.

The ER nurse set up a tray of equipment to use when the baby came. Another nurse was setting up a portable infant incubator near June's stretcher. Her dad stepped back when her mom showed up. Through wet eyes, June saw Kim at the foot of the bed. She smiled and waved goodbye.

"Mom, take Dad somewhere before he faints."

"We're staying. But who's going to do the delivery?"

"I am," Divya said, rushing in. She was dressed in scrubs from the other hospital.

"Where have you been?" June asked, trying not to sound irritated.

With gloves on her hands, Divya tossed the sheet back to examine June. "I was just finishing with a case in town when my office called about your emergency. I never drove so fast in all my life."

Divya didn't like the crowded trauma bay and shooed several people away. June, panting and sweating, watching her parents leave.

“Mom, get my phone and call Jack. He’ll want to know. And get Amy on the phone.”

She barely heard her mother make the promise, instead feeling her mind swirl. She got lost in a confusion of thoughts and memories, of the rushed trip across the island in the back of a police car, the fistfight with Scanlon, the discussions on the phone, of breakfast. Voices spoke to her in each passing scene: Kim, the cop, the clerk in Honolulu, her mother and father, Amy. Piercing through them all came one other voice.

“It’s time now,” the benevolent voice said. It was the same voice as she’d heard many times before. “She’s ready to meet her family.”

“I know,” June said quietly, getting the attention of both Divya and the nurse at the side. “We’re ready for her, too.”

“Know what?” Divya asked, getting into a surgical gown for the delivery.

“It’s time,” June said.

She panted through a heavy contraction, her knees bent and feet braced against the pad of the stretcher. Divya told her to take some slow deep breaths and wait for her prompts.

“Forget that. She’s coming…now…”

Divya pulled back the sheet covering June from the waist down. June gripped the stretcher pad and panted.

“I can see the top of the baby’s head, June. Next time you feel a contraction start, just push with everything you’ve got.”

“That’s right now…”

***

June was drenched in sweat, and could barely control her breathing. It wasn’t just pressure, or contractions, but pain, sheer pain. There was an over-whelming sense of doom, that something was horribly wrong. It was all going so fast, the crowning so quick after her water breaking, followed by the ride in the back of a squad car. Her pediatrician had been late and she was having her baby in an Emergency Room, not in L and D. Making things worse, Amy wasn't there and she was missing Jack more than ever. Nothing was going as planned.

"Push June. You have to push as hard as you can."

Looking through the sweat-sodden hair matted to her face, tears streaming down her cheeks, June clenched her teeth, furrowed her brow, and grabbed a hold of the siderails of the stretcher, bearing down.

"Harder, June! Almost there!"

At the height of the crushing pain in her belly, she pushed with all her might. The room swirled, her vision dark and narrow. Feeling she might explode, there was relief just as she was about to black out.

Light-headed and her mind swirling, June heard a baby cry. The high-pitched sounds brought her mind around again. She tried focusing her eyes at the foot of the bed where Divya stood, working busily. Someone standing next to her said to take a few deep breaths. They tried putting an oxygen mask on her face but June swatted it away. The baby's cries turned to infantile wails. Finally finding her focus, she saw a wet, pink head.

"Give me my baby," she said softly, reaching her sweaty arms forward.

The nurse put a warm baby blanket over the baby once Divya put her on June's chest. They were still joined by the cord.

"Mom," June tried to call out, but couldn't find a strong voice. "Get my mom," she told the nurse.

"I have to cut her loose, June."

"Just a minute," June said. She held the baby on her chest and felt the warm damp cord with her hand. Mixed in with the sweat on her face were a thousand tears. She kissed the baby several times, and held her close to her face, listening to her soft attempts to cry. "Okay."

Divya put clamps on the cord and cut with a stout pair of scissors, taking the cord off June's chest.

"Hi, little girl," June whispered. "So, you're the one who's been kicking me all this time?"

The baby was pointing with one finger, her eyes closed, her mouth in something of a pucker. June couldn't resist planting several more kisses on her wet face.

"I love you, little one. Always remember that."

Mabel and Tak came from around the curtain, beaming. The baby got more kisses.

"Did you get a hold of Jack?"

"A staffer said was in a meeting. I wasn't sure if I was supposed to explain what was going on," her father said.

"Mom, did you call Amy?"

"I need to do an APGAR score," the nurse said quietly. "And get her in the incubator and cleaned off."

"She's a ten."

It was an internal contest of wills, but she let the nurse have her baby, watching as she was placed in the warm incubator next to her stretcher. She smiled and more tears streamed from her eyes.

"Here's Amy," Mabel said, handing June the phone.

"Hi Mommy," Amy said on the phone. It was on speaker. "You did it."

"She did it. You should see her."

"Mom already sent a pic. She has a dimple, just like her beautiful mother. What's her name?"

"What did you decide?" Divya asked, holding a swaddled baby in her arms.

"Give me Melanie," June said, reaching up again.

Getting the baby, she turned on her side to cuddle.

"Melanie Aiko Haunani Kim Kato-Melendez, I'd like you to meet your family."

"How many babies did you have?" Amy asked from the phone.

"It turns out I'm the sensible one in the family, having only one at a time."

"June, it's Jack on the phone," her father said, holding out the cell phone. They all watched closely as she took the phone from him.

"Is that…" Divya asked, whispering.

"Yes," Tak whispered back.

"Hey, Daddy," June muttered into the phone. "You have one more reason to save the world."

Divya took over at massaging June's belly, and took a quick look under the sheet, while June filled in Jack on the details of their baby.

"June, we should get Melanie over to Maternity so a pediatrician can check her out."

June ended her call and gave Melanie back to the nurse, who put her in the incubator for the trip to the Maternity Ward.

"We still have more work to do here, June."

"Dad, get lost. We have lady things to do now. You go with him, Mom. Go with Melanie, make sure she doesn't get lost." She wiped her face. "She doesn't know her way around Maui yet."

June turned over onto her back.

"What happened?" Divya asked her. "I heard something about a police car?"

What had occurred barely an hour before seemed like a lifetime ago to June. "Yeah, I guess I can't do anything the easy way. And I broke a few rules."

She told an abbreviated form of her trip to town, to go to the police station, and then to get her nails done and buy a new blouse. Right then, she couldn't believe she had been lured into Marilyn's office so easily, and felt embarrassed by it.

"You punched that woman?" Divya asked, massaging June's belly again.

"Not much choice. She had a syringe full of succinylcholine in her hand, aimed at me. Then the cops got there, and Kim came in to help. Somewhere along the way, I was pushed and my water broke." That's when she remembered Kim and wondered where she had gone to.

"Okay, just one more question," Divya said. "Was that really, well, Jack, you know, on the phone?"

"Yep."

"Where was he? I mean, we didn't interrupt anything, did we?"

"In the Oval. Kinda hard not to interrupt anything important with him."

"Wow," was all the young obstetrician said.

June's hospital gown was changed, along with the sheets on the stretcher. The curtain was pulled back, and she saw Detective Atkins waiting nearby.

"You've been waiting all this time?"

He nodded. "How was your baby?"

"Go see her! My parents went with her to maternity."

Two nurses were waiting to wheel her to the maternity ward, but the cop waved them away.

"We should talk. I need a statement from you about what happened back in town."

"Does that mean you saw the report I filed earlier today?" June asked.

"I did, and believe it or not, I've been investigating ever since we spoke a few days ago."

June went through the scene in Marilyn's little office as best she could, the officer taking notes. She then gave what she'd discovered about Marilyn's past, and what she had learned at the morgue. It was basically the same report she'd given at the police station earlier in the day.

"That drug in the syringe, you saw her take it right from the vial?" the police officer asked, getting back to the present situation.

"It looked like a Sux vial. They normally have a bright orange label. Anyway, she didn't deny it, and…" She looked at her upper arm. "…you can see where she grazed me with the needle."

He leaned over for a better look, took a picture with his phone, and made a few notes on his pad.

"If you need another witness, I'm sure Kim heard it from out on the sidewalk."

"Kim?"

"Kim. She works in the hair salon a few doors down from Marilyn's office. She came into the office at the same time as the officers." The officer who drove June to the hospital came to her bedside just then, also taking notes. "Officer, you'll know Kim when you see her. She was the one that came here in your car, in the back seat with me."

The officer lowered his pad and looked at June hard in the eyes. “I’m sorry. Maybe I’m confused. You were the only one in the back seat.”

“What? No, a lady named Kim was back there with me. She helped me with contractions the whole way here.”

“I’m sorry. It was just you and me in the car coming here. You told me to come here, made some phone calls, but most of the time you were kind of out of it, just talking to yourself.”

“Wait. What do you mean, talking to myself?” June asked, confused.

“Maybe like you were having a conversation with yourself, like how someone talks in their sleep.”

June frowned, more confused than ever. “Is there anything else? I want to go see my baby.”

“I should have the name and contact number of the father,” Atkins said.

“He’s not on the island right now.”

“Maybe just his name for our records?”

There was no way she was going to out the identity of Melanie’s father, not as President, anyway. Instead of calling him Jack, as America knew him by, she went with his birth name. “J. Sebastian Melendez. But if you go to maternity, you can get my parents’ names and numbers. They live with me.”

Getting the high-sign from the detective and police officer, the nurses pushed June down the hall to the maternity ward.

“Did you guys see a slender Korean lady in the ER a little while ago, waiting for me?” she asked the nurses as they went down the hall.

"We just started work a few minutes ago. But we heard your baby is super cute!"

"Thanks."

"Really long, too. She'll be tall."

"It felt like there was a crowd in there."

She was still confused when they got to the maternity ward. When she saw her family waiting for her, gathered around the hospital bassinette, she forgot all about the officer's questions and Kim. All she was interested in was Melanie.

***

While the baby had her first meal, her parents got ready to go home so June could be alone with Melanie.

"Mom, wait a minute. I want to talk with you a minute more, alone."

June had already had time to clean up and move into a formal bed, had a meal, and felt refreshed. It was the baby's turn for a meal at June's breast.

"What is it, Dear? From what I can see, you're doing that right."

"No, something else. In the ER, when you first got here, did you see a Korean woman standing around, skinny, pretty? Acting like she was waiting for me?"

"So many Asians here. I was just looking for you. Why?"

"You didn't see the same lady that did my hair the other day?"

Mabel frowned. "I told you before, there was only one stylist there that day, and she was with me while you napped."

"Really?"

"We've already been over that. But why'd you name the baby Kim?" her mother asked.

Melanie had finishing feeding and was asleep, but June hugged the baby close.

"I'm not sure why." June told her mother the story of the stylist rushing into Marilyn's office, and coming with her to the hospital in the back seat of the police car. "But the cop said I was alone in the back seat on the way here. I don't understand."

Mabel took June's free hand into hers. "It's a pretty name. Nice to keep it in the family."

More confusion was setting in, June trying to chase it away again. "Mom, I need to get some sleep. Make sure you guys get dinner tonight, okay?"

Chapter Five

More than a week had passed since Melanie was born, and a semblance of routine had settled in at home. Flowers and gifts had arrived from Jack and Amy, more for Melanie than June. Somehow, June's hospital work had become a million miles away. Clinic patients were rescheduled, and she didn't care when. Her sole focus in life was on Melanie.

"What time are they supposed to get here?" June asked for the hundredth time that morning.

"Any time now," her mother told her. Per their latest routine, Mabel had given Melanie her morning bath while June showered. Once she was ready, the baby was given another feeding. It had become something of a slow motion relay race in the house, Melanie going from one set of arms to another, until it was decided it was time for a meal or nap. And June was never far away from either of those.

With Melanie cuddled close to her in bed, June was barely awake when she heard someone come into the house. It was Amy, and she hadn't come alone.

"Is that my favorite niece?" Amy said, cracking the bedroom door open, peeking in.

"The only one you have."

Amy sat on the bed, the baby not stirring. She stared down at her, and June could tell her sister wanted to hold Melanie.

"Are you going to hold her, or not?"

"Give her to me," Amy demanded. Like an expert mother, Amy swept up the baby in her arms.

"You had to bring the whole family?" June asked.

"It's all the girls have talked about, their new cousin. They're still trying to figure it out."

"You took them out of school for a few days to come here?"

"What are they going to miss? Practice counting to ten?"

"How's Mick?"

"As in, why'd I have to bring him?"

"Light-years ago, Sis."

"Everything is great. He's good with the girls, he manages the stores well, and he's a good husband."

"Wow. That's exciting," June said drolly.

"That's life in the big city, Babe."

"In Orange County, anyway."

There was a tiny knock at the door, and June knew who it had to be. "Come on in and meet Melanie, girls!"

Her nieces and Amy's husband Mick came in. Suddenly there was a crowd, and Melanie picked up on it, responding by fussing. Amy kept the baby in her arms, cuddling and cooing at her.

"Mom said she came pretty fast?" Amy asked quietly.

"I guess I was in labor all morning but wasn't smart enough to know it. Then when my water broke, things progressed faster than I ever thought they would. There weren't any ambulances available, and me being stubborn…"

"You insisted on being brought from town all the way over here. Which took how long?"

"I don't know. An hour? I was pretty out of it by then, talking to people that weren't there. Well, as people say here, Maui time took over."

"I heard about that," Amy said, giving Melanie back to her mother. After her blanket was adjusted, she was handed over to Ruka and Koemi, so they could meet their new cousin.

"That's the way it was for me, too," Amy said. "Having breakfast one minute, and the next thing I knew I was in the hospital, tossing accusations at everybody I saw."

"A moment none of us will ever forget, Sis," June said with a grin.

"Then it was wham, bam, thank you ma'am, and I had two hungry kids."

"Must be a Kato family trait. We can't be bothered with wasting time on labor and childbirth."

After June's twin nieces cradled Melanie on their laps for a few minutes, and Mick held her for a moment, June knew it was time for Melanie's first expedition into public. Other than the mile ride home in the car, she hadn't been beyond her crib, tub, or June's arms.

It had been a group effort of Mabel, Tak, and Mick to get the baby seat secured in Amy's full-sized rental sedan. While they took Melanie on her first trip out, the rest of the group was going to lunch elsewhere.

As Amy drove, June pointed the way through town, the way she wanted to go.

"The house is cute," Amy said.

"Once the addition is done, we'll have a little more breathing room."

"Mom and Dad are going to stay with you?"

"That's the plan, at least until I kill them in their sleep. It's already getting claustrophobic."

"Built-in babysitters," Amy said. "Melanie needs someone during the day while you're at work. Believe it or not, Mom and Dad can deal with a baby."

June pointed Amy to drive along the coast highway, wind from off the ocean buffeting the car. She looked at Melanie dozing in the back seat. "How in the world did I ever accomplish that?"

"And somehow, without planning it out years in advance," Amy said. "What ever happened with the lady and some scorpions? I never did get much of an explanation from Mom."

"It was the stupidest crime wave ever. Some dope set up shop as a so-called birth angel, trying to bilk money out of desperate pregnant women with fake aura massages and phony fortune telling."

"And that led to murder?"

"Several of them. Once the women were on to her scam, they reported her to the police, doctors, the media, everybody. Nobody listened, thinking they were whack-jobs. The police have done an investigation, learning that somehow she was able to inject them with a drug that paralyzed their respiratory muscles, then hid the injection site with a scorpion sting. When each woman was eventually found, she was either already dead or so close she couldn't be saved. Except two."

June went on to explain about the woman that had been brought in to the ER by the housekeeper, one of the survivors in the group. She was the one who gave the last pieces of the puzzle, and eventually identified Marilyn as the culprit.

"But how did she figure out how to do that, with the drug?" Amy asked.

"She had been a nurse, and lost her job after diverting drugs." June was reluctant to go on, since the next part really was her fault, the part that started the fight between her and Marilyn. "I called her on it."

"Once you had a suspicion something was going on, why didn't you call the police? You just wanted to go off on one of your little causes again?" Amy asked.

"No. First, I talked to a detective, and he was less than interested in investigating. On the morning all this happened, I called the police and they said to come in and file a report. So, like a good little citizen, that's what I did. Then I went to town to get some fresh air. It was only a few minutes later when I saw that woman at her office and got all tangled up in her sick little web."

"Just like always. But what I don't understand is why you went there right after filing a report with the police?" Amy asked.

"Dumbest reason ever. I looked like crap in those days, and thought I might get my nails done, and buy something pretty to wear, or at least something that fit. Her office was right in the middle of a cute little shopping district. When I went past, she just sort of lured me in."

"And you were going to be her next victim. But the woman, the perp, was so vindictive of women reporting her to the authorities, she killed them?"

"They've done a psych evaluation on her. Apparently, she's psycho and has been for a long time. That's the real reason the state pulled her license, preventing her from ever working as a health care professional again."

"Which is why she made up the phony birth angel practitioner bit," Amy said. "I know it's bad for the other families, but at least you survived, Babe, and that's what counts to me."

"She's been stopped, anyway."

"Let me see if I understand this," Amy said. "You were nine months pregnant and went to confront someone you thought was a murderer, on her home turf?"

"Right."

"Once you get there, you picked a fight with her while you're in labor?"

"Yep."

"And when your water broke, you beat her up?"

"I guess you could put it that way."

"But Dad told me how you freaked out when you found a scorpion eating a centipede on the bathroom floor."

June laughed. "Kinda ironic, huh?"

She considered telling Amy about Kim, her appearance in the police car and disappearance later. It just sounded like crazy talk. When she had brought it up with Divya Gill, her obstetrician, that was the explanation she had got, that she had probably suffered from some prenatal psychosis, not terribly uncommon for women that worked full-term in demanding professions.

But prenatal psychosis or elaborate hallucinations didn't explain why June learned so much about her Korean grandmother, her history, her name, even that she had a dimple like her own. None of it was explainable at all, and her mother denied ever telling her about it.

"Who is this we're visiting today?" Amy asked. "Some Hawaiian lady?"

"Auntie Haunani."

"One of the namesakes of Melanie?"

"A few weeks before my due date, I was getting really anxious. She calmed me down, explained some stuff, taught me how to deal with poisonous bugs, how to keep them out of the house. For that, she deserves a part of the pie."

"I saw the funnels, and heard about the rock you keep under the crib."

"And there hasn't been a single bug in the house since then. Plus, she knows stuff."

"What kind of stuff?"

"Never mind. I'll explain later, if you still want to hear about it after meeting her."

June pointed Amy to the cane haul road to follow to Auntie Haunani's house. The road had dried and the rainwater puddles long gone by then.

"Down here? Is this okay? No dogs to chase us away?"

June looked in the bag from the butcher shop, where she bought the beef bone for Ili the dog. "That's what this is for."

Amy pulled into the gravel area in front of Haunani's house and parked. Ili gave a few half-hearted barks before getting a command in Hawaiian from inside the house. Once again, no other cars were around, even though there was enough space to park several vehicles.

"She's expecting us, right?" Amy asked, shutting off the engine.

They both stared out the windshield at the house while Ili trotted up to the car at June's side.

"She said come anytime. But I have the idea she's expecting us." June opened her window and gave the dog the bone. Out of the car, she went to the back seat to get Melanie. "Come on, you're going to like your new Auntie Haunani."

More from Kay Hadashi

The June Kato Intrigue Series

Kimono Suicide

Stalking Silk

Yakuza Lover

Deadly Contact

Orchids and Ice

Broken Protocol

The Island Breeze Series

Island Breeze

Honolulu Hostage

Maui Time

Big Island Business

Adrift

Molokai Madness

Ghost of a Chance

The Melanie Kato Adventure Series

Away

Faith

Risk

Quest

Mission

Secrets

Future

Kahuna

Directive

Nano

The Maui Mystery Series

A Wave of Murder
A Hole in One Murder
A Moonlit Murder
A Spa Full of Murder
A Down to Earth Murder
A Haunted Murder
A Plan for Murder
A Misfortunate Murder
A Quest for Murder
A Game of Murder

The Honolulu Thriller Series

Interisland Flight
Kama'aina Revenge
Tropical Revenge
Waikiki Threat
Rainforest Rescue

Maile Spencer Honolulu Tour Guide Mysteries

AWOL at Ala Moana
Baffled at the Beach
Coffee in the Canal
Dead at Diamond Head
Honey of a Hurricane
Keepers of the Kingdom
Malice in the Palace
Peril at the Potluck